HOOP GIRLZ

ALSO BY LUCY JANE BLEDSOE

The Big Bike Race
illustrated by Sterling Brown

Tracks in the Snow

Cougar Canyon

HOOP
GIRLZ

Lucy Jane
Bledsoe

Holiday House / New York

Library of Congress Cataloging-in-Publication Data
Bledsoe, Lucy Jane.
Hoop girlz / by Lucy Jane Bledsoe.—1st ed.
p. cm.
Summary: When eleven-year-old River, who is crazy about basketball, is not chosen to
play in the tournament set up in the town of Azalea, Oregon, she decides to organize a
team of her own and accepts the help of her older brother.
ISBN 0-8234-1691-7
[1. Basketball—Fiction. 2. Teamwork (Sports)—Fiction. 3. Self-confidence—Fiction.
4. Brothers and sisters—Fiction.] I. Title.

PZ7.B6168 Ho 2002
[Fic]—dc21   2001059451

FOR KELSEY

CONTENTS

HOOP
GIRLZ

1. WANTED: BASKETBALL TALENT

River ran from the car to the high school gym. In spite of the pelting rain, she dribbled her basketball the whole way, dodging around the parking lot puddles and charging full speed until she reached the gym door. There she stopped, hugging her wet basketball.

Out here was the dark, wet night. Pouring rain. Strong winds off the nearby Pacific. But inside . . .

River pushed open the door. The band was blaring out the school song. Their trumpets and trombones reflected gold light. The sound of high-top sneakers pounding the court echoed off the walls as the two teams warmed up. Balls boinged off the floor, slapped into hands, swished through the nets. A wild kind of sweat and muscle dance.

River climbed the bleachers and found an empty row, then leaned forward to watch the high school girls warm up. Her brother, Zack, and neighbor, Kammie Wilder, scooted in next to her.

This was the very gym where Emily Hargraves, last year's MVP of the Women's National Basketball Association, got her start. Across the main street in town, the mayor had stretched a banner which read: AZALEA, OREGON, HOMETOWN OF EMILY HARGRAVES, MOST VALUABLE PLAYER OF THE WNBA. Every day on her way to school, River stopped directly under the banner, no matter how hard it was raining. Every day she closed her eyes and said an affirmation. "I, River Borowitz-Jacobs, am going to play for the WNBA." If Emily Hargraves had made it, so could she.

There were obstacles, though. For one, her height was only average for an eleven-year-old girl. Zack, who was fourteen, had the same problem, but he said they were still both young enough for growth spurts.

It wasn't just her height, though. River didn't look anything like a basketball player. Emily Hargraves was tall, with honey-colored hair and high, peachy cheekbones. Her eyes were a determined gray, and even her square jaw said *win*. River, on the other hand, looked like something that could blow away in the wind. Her parents should have called her Leaf. Her black hair was thin and wispy. Her eyes were green with flecks of brown, and she had freckles everywhere.

Zack, who looked exactly like his sister, said that their greatest obstacle was their parents. Lawrence Jacobs was a photographer; Carolyn Borowitz was a ceramic artist. They didn't believe in sports. "They don't believe in anything," Zack complained, "except art and organic vegetables."

The Azalea High School team finished running layups and now were shooting from around the key. A couple of hotshots made passes behind their backs. One girl changed directions by dribbling the ball between her legs.

Kammie Wilder tapped River's arm.

"I'm concentrating," River said.

The team ran off the court and into a huddle. The cheerleading squad cartwheeled onto the floor and began their routine.

"Roger is gonna buy me sneakers just like Emily Hargraves's," Kammie said.

River looked at her brother.

He shook his head without taking his eyes off the court. Kammie's stepdad was an out-of-work logger. He couldn't afford expensive sneakers.

"Yesterday when I was shooting baskets in the gym," Kammie went on, nudging River again to get her attention, "a scout from the WNBA was watching me."

River looked to Zack again.

"No way," he said.

"He said he could probably offer me a contract this year."

"He did not!" River chimed in.

"Bets?"

"How much?"

"You don't believe me."

River shrugged. WNBA scouts looking at eleven-year-olds? No way.

"He did," Kammie insisted.

Near the end of the game, which Azalea was winning by a landslide, as usual, the other team called a time-out. Both teams went into huddles. Kammie jumped to her feet and pointed at a very tall man walking in front of the bleachers. "There he is!" she shouted. "The man who was scouting me."

"That's just that new girl, Rochelle Glover's father," River informed her. But then she remembered—people did say that Wally Glover had played for the New York Knicks. Years ago. No one had heard of him, but that didn't mean anything. Lots of people play professional basketball who never become famous.

"That's the guy," Kammie said quietly. "He said I had tremendous potential."

"That's cool," River said to end the conversation. She wanted to concentrate on the high school players' moves. They were awesome, totally awesome.

After the game, Zack told the girls to hurry. Their parents were picking them up in the parking lot. River took her time, anyway. She loved the stuffy smell of the gym after a game. She liked watching the fans hugging the athletes, shaking hands with the coach, celebrating yet another win.

Basketball was the best thing about Azalea. Both the boys' and girls' high school teams won all their games. Not much else happened in town. The place used to be a booming logging town, but now it was full of out-of-work loggers, and a few artists. Most of the buildings in the tiny downtown were empty. Some people called Azalea a ghost town. There were even stories that the abandoned mansion, where the timber baron once lived, was haunted.

"River, come on," Zack said.

She filed out of the gym following the rest of the crowd. The new girl's dad stood in the doorway, handing out flyers and creating a bottleneck.

"Nice to see you again," he said. River looked up quickly. He was speaking to Kammie. "I want to see you at tryouts, young lady."

"I'll be there," Kammie nearly shouted.

River watched Kammie shake hands with Wally Glover.

Then turning to River with her snaggle-toothed smile, Kammie practically pasted the flyer on River's face, saying, "See, I told you so!"

River took the flyer.

Scouting Players for the WNBA
Wanted: *Basketball talent for a sixth-grade girls' team. Only girls who are willing to work very hard and play to win need try out.* **Goal**: *First place in an Oregon Coast Tournament in March.* **Tryouts**: *Friday afternoon, 3:30 P.M. sharp.* **Bonus**: *Emily Hargraves will attend the tournament and select the MVP, who will win a free place at her basketball camp this summer.*

Kammie pointed to *MVP* and said, "That's me. I'm going to be the Most Valuable Player and go to Emily Hargraves's basketball camp this summer. Hah!"

Oh no, it's not *you,* River vowed silently to herself. *It's me.*

Once they were in the car, Kammie snatched back the flyer. "Look, Carolyn, I'm being recruited for the WNBA."

River's mom read the flyer out loud and

then said, "Sixth grade is just too young. It's bad enough they get so serious in junior high. This is ridiculous."

"It's just one tournament," her dad commented.

"But look at the wording of this flyer. 'Play to win,'" she quoted the flyer. "For goodness sake. Kids should play to have fun. And this part about scouting for the WNBA! Why, he's misleading the children."

"No, he's not!" River cried. "Emily Hargraves plays for the WNBA. And she'll be at the tournament. Basically, that makes her a scout."

Carolyn Jacobs sighed and said to her husband, "See what I mean?"

"Get a grip, Mom," Zack said without turning his gaze from the window. "In case you haven't noticed, basketball builds character. Which is a lot more than can be said for slapping wet hunks of clay."

"I'm hungry!" Kammie announced. "Let's stop at your house and get something to eat."

Carolyn Jacobs smiled. "Why not? It's a Saturday night. We can have a party."

River reached into the front seat and took the flyer from her mom's lap. By now they were out on the highway, passing the haunted mansion, where there were no streetlights at all. Zack reached up and snapped on the overhead light. Together they reread the flyer.

River felt something inside her sharpen to a point as she whispered, "River Borowitz-Jacobs, sixth grade girls' MVP of the Oregon Coast." She closed her eyes and imagined playing one-on-one with Emily Hargraves at basketball camp. *Yes.*

2. TEAM TRYOUTS

On Friday afternoon about half of the girls in the sixth-grade class came to tryouts. Even Erica, who always held a cell phone to her ear. Even Wilfred, who was frightened of everything, including paper airplanes. Even Jennifer who, judging by how recklessly she drove her wheelchair in the school halls, would be a danger on the court.

River dressed quickly and stepped into the gym a full twenty minutes early. To impress Coach Glover, she ran a few warm-up laps. Each time she passed under a basket, she leaped up and tried to tag the net. She never came close, but she figured it looked good. Then she did one lap running backward because Zack told her that his coach had them do that.

Next she began warming up her shot. She ran some layups, missing only one. She shot from different spots around the key, nailing most of them. She backed up and tried shooting from the three-point line.

"Air ball!" Kammie crowed, trotting onto the court. She snatched the rebound and toed the three-point line herself. Lowering the ball between her bent knees, Kammie hurled it toward the basket underhand. It arched high and fell through the hoop. "All net," she hollered.

"That was luck," River told her. "You've never hit one before!"

River noticed the new girl, the coach's daughter, standing on the sideline watching. She was tall with white blond hair tied back in a ponytail.

Kammie noticed her, too. She tossed her the ball and said, "One on one, play to ten. Bet I can beat you."

Rochelle shrugged. Like a pale giraffe, she walked lankily into the key. The top of Kammie's head didn't even reach her shoulders. Rochelle held the ball up and popped in two points.

Kammie laughed.

Until Rochelle did it again—shot right over her head for another two points.

Kammie wiped her hands on her shorts. She bit her bottom lip.

Rochelle was as cool as rain. River noticed that she wore the very sneakers Kammie wanted, the exact kind that Emily Hargraves wore. Then River saw that the number on Rochelle's T-shirt was Emily's number. The girl acted like she already owned the title of MVP.

In two long steps, Rochelle was past Kammie for a layup.

River cheered silently when Rochelle missed the next shot and Kammie snatched the rebound. Kammie might be short, but she was fast and had great ball-handling skills. She started dribbling in circles around Rochelle. More girls had joined River on the sidelines, and they all laughed. When Rochelle looked over at her dad, Kammie drove to the bucket.

"Gotcha!" Kammie yelled.

She managed to drive past Rochelle two more times to tie up the score. Kammie's face was red and her eyes were like two beams of light.

At the top of the key, she held the ball over her head. Rochelle took a couple of steps back because Kammie had driven past her so many times now. Kammie saw the opportunity and put up a long shot. Gold!

Kammie shouted, "I'm ahead, 8 to 6! Kammie Wilder, MVP!"

Coach Glover blew his whistle.

"Listen up, ladies." His voice was deep and hoarse, as if he'd been shouting for hours already. "Time for the serious work to begin. Line up on the end line."

River jogged to the end line. At last, she thought, serious hoops.

"That's not fair!" Kammie protested, squeezing into the line of girls next to River. "I would have beat her if he hadn't interrupted the game."

"Shh!" River warned.

"She doesn't have any skills," Kammie continued, loud enough for everyone to hear. "It's just because she's so tall."

"Be quiet."

Coach Glover paced along the lineup, looking over each girl as if he was trying to decide which one to buy. River straightened her back.

"Basketball," he suddenly boomed, "is a metaphor for life. Who can tell me what a metaphor is?"

"Like an example!" Kammie shouted out.

"Rochelle?" Coach Glover called on his daughter.

"Yes, sir. A metaphor is an example of something. It means that basketball can teach us how to live life."

"Exactly."

"That's what I said," Kammie said under her breath to River.

"*Shh,*" River told her again.

"To win in basketball, as in life, you have to work extremely hard and make sacrifices. I'm going to be selecting a squad of eight girls who are willing to make this commitment. You better believe I'll be looking at your skills today during tryouts, but I'll also be looking at your attitudes. I'm going to carry just eight girls because I want only the very best. However, any girls who don't make the A-Team can play for the B-Team. We will find a parent to coach that team. Have I made myself clear?"

River nodded. A couple of the girls said, "Yeah."

Wally Glover shouted, *"Have I made myself clear?"*

Wilfred, the girl who jumped when you said *good morning,* bleated a little "aaah" of fright. Even Kammie flinched. Everyone looked at one another nervously.

Finally, Rochelle said, "Yes, sir."

Just then, a shrill purr vibrated the gym air. Erica ran to the bleachers, pulling her cell phone from her gym bag. "Hello?" she said. "Hi, Mom."

Coach Glover drew a breath and placed his hands on his hips, his elbows jutting straight out. River could tell that he wasn't even going to bother chewing out Erica. She was a good player, but no way was she going to make the team now.

Coach Glover continued, "We have exactly two months, so there isn't a minute to waste. I'll be setting up some practice games between now and then, but our goal is winning the Oregon Coast Tournament in the middle of March. *Not* third place. *Not* second place. *First place.* Have I made myself clear?"

"Yes, *sir,*" all the girls answered. Erica, who was back on the end line, saluted as well.

"Excellent. What is our goal in March?"

"First place," they all shouted.

Coach Glover smiled. "Excellent."

He was going to be very tough, River thought, but that was exactly the kind of coach she needed if she was going to make the WNBA. Satin jerseys! Brass music! Stomping fans! She imagined herself driving to the hoop for a crucial two points, the gym exploding with cheers.

"Coach Glover?" she asked.

"What is it?"

"Do we get uniforms?"

"Of course."

"What color?"

"This is not a fashion club, young lady. This is a basketball club." He paced along the line of girls, stopping right in front of River, who felt her face burning. "To achieve our goal, I'll need girls who are capable of extreme concentration and dedication. Those who make the A-Team will be expected to practice daily after school. The only accepted excuse will be illness. Not late homework. And not"—he turned to address the parents in the bleachers—"family vacations. *Have I made myself clear?*"

"Yes, sir!" the girls all shouted.

"Suicides!" Coach Glover ordered. No one moved. River knew about suicides from Zack, but the other girls looked frightened until Coach Glover explained. They were to sprint to quarter court, touch the floor, and sprint back to the end line. Then they were to sprint to mid court, touch the floor, and sprint back. Finally, they were to sprint to the far end line, touch the floor, and sprint back. That was a suicide.

He blew his whistle and the girls took off. By the time River finished the suicide, her lungs felt as if they would explode. Some of the slower girls were still jogging back to the end line when Coach Glover shouted, "Again!" and blew his whistle.

"Wait a minute," River called out to him. "Jennifer isn't finished."

Jennifer was still on the far end line. She bent forward in her wheelchair, touched the line, then headed back toward the group, her arms working so fast on the wheels they were a blur.

Ignoring River, Coach Glover blew his whistle again and shouted, "Go!"

The girls took off on the next set of sprints, dodging around Jennifer as she finished her first set. It gave River a funny feeling to go flying past her. But Coach Glover must know what he was doing. After all, this was a professional team in training.

On the way back from the next suicide, River found herself heading straight for Jennifer, who was rolling in the opposite direction. They both moved to get out of the other's way—but in the same direction. River's foot caught in the wheel of Jennifer's chair and she crashed to the floor.

"Watch where you're going!" Jennifer shouted.

"You were zigzagging all over the court!" River shot back.

"I had to dodge everyone else!"

When their eyes met, they both started

giggling. River laughed so hard, she rolled over on her back and held her stomach.

"Get up," Jennifer said suddenly. Coach Glover was waiting for the two of them with his hands on his hips. River jumped up and grabbed the handles on Jennifer's chair.

"Hold on," she said, unable to control a fresh bout of giggling. The two girls finished their suicide together, with River pushing.

Next, Coach Glover had the girls do lay-ups. River made sure to get in some of her trick shots, like crossing under the basket and laying the ball up from under the opposite side. Once she tried a hook shot, which bounced off the backboard and flew into the bleachers. Jennifer and Erica cracked up, which got River laughing, too.

Coach Glover blew his whistle. "You girls have a joke you'd like to share with the rest of us?"

River shook her head.

Jennifer stared straight ahead.

But Erica launched into explaining, "See, it was the way that River tried to show off her hook shot, but it went flying—"

The shrill whistle cut her off.

"Well, he asked," Erica said.

"He meant we were supposed to shut up," Jennifer explained in a fierce whisper.

Next, Coach Glover had the girls run three-on-three passing drills.

"No, no, no!" Coach Glover shouted, stepping into the key. "When you make a pass, be decisive." He bounce passed the ball to Wilfred so hard that she froze with fright. It bonked off her forehead. When tears filled her eyes, he chucked her under the chin, sort of hard, and said, "Go ahead and have a seat for a while." He gave her a little shove toward the bleachers.

"Another competitor bites the dust," Kammie said.

"He's mean," one girl said, and walked right off the court and into the locker room.

Coach Glover didn't seem to even notice her. After the passing drill, he began a demonstration of how to defend an opponent. He jumped into the key, his big feet thudding on the shiny floorboards. All the girls trying out for the team stood in front of him, watching.

All, that is, except for Erica. She'd crept in back of him and began imitating his every move. If he scooted to the right, she scooted to the right. If he shot his arms in the air, she shot hers up. Finally she bunched her tongue under her upper lip, scowled hard, and held her ears out in her famous gorilla imitation. She reached one hand under her armpit and scratched, making a soft *"hoo hoo hoo"* gorilla sound. That's when Coach Glover turned around.

"Whoops," Erica said, straightening out her face.

River felt another wave of giggles rise up in her.

"The drama club," Coach Glover told Erica, "might be able to use your talents, young lady, but not a ball club. Take the bench."

A few minutes later, when Coach Glover told them to pair up for one on one, River looked around for a partner. Forget Rochelle. Way too tall. Erica was on the bench. She'd feel bad winning against Jennifer. River started to make her way toward Sarah, but Marianne beat her. So she headed for Jeannie, but Jeannie got tapped by Rochelle. Who was left?

Kammie.

There were six hoops in the gym and the pairs of girls divided up among them. Coach Glover held a pen and clipboard. As the girls began their games of one on one, he took notes.

River stood with the ball at the top of the key. Kammie stepped up to play defense. "Go ahead," she said, waving her hands in River's face. "Try and get around me."

River bent her knees and made like she was going to take a jump shot from right there, at the top of the key. Kammie went for the fake and leaped to block the shot. River ducked under Kammie's right armpit and drove to the basket for an easy layup.

"Two-zero," River said, glancing around to see if Coach Glover had been watching. Unfortunately he was on the other side of the court.

"You won't get past me a second time," Kammie said as they took their positions at the top of the key again.

This time River drove hard to the left, her weak side. Kammie reached out and slapped the ball. River looked at her empty hands.

"Hah!" Kammie flashed her cocky grin and held the ball over her head.

River jumped and snatched the ball back. She drove to the basket for a second easy two points.

"Four-zero!" she said loudly this time.

She looked around for Coach Glover. He was just walking over to their game with his clipboard. Kammie wasn't grinning anymore.

Here it goes, River thought. Time to shine.

She faked a jumper from the top of the key. Then she sidestepped to the corner and quickly popped up a shot. It hit the rim . . . and dropped in. "Six-zero!"

Coach Glover took a note.

As River took the ball to the top of the key, she did some quick math in her head—in eleven years she'd be ready to play in the WNBA. Where she'd have to be good enough to play against people like Emily Hargraves. River glanced at the coach again. He was waiting for her to do something with the ball.

The pressure made her arms and legs feel heavy. The hoop rim looked far away. She tossed the ball toward the basket.

And missed. Kammie got the rebound.

"Watch this," Kammie said to Coach Glover. She drove right past River and made a layup.

Kammie drove by her again and scored. Kammie was fast, but River had stopped her before. Now it felt as if her feet were glued to the floor. She just wanted to give up.

After Kammie popped two points from the side, River finally got the rebound. It was 6 to 6. She took the ball to the top of the key. She cut to the right and made a short jumper. But she missed the next one, and Kammie got the ball.

Kammie backed up to the three-point line and grinned at the watching coach. Then to River she said, "You thought my three-pointer was luck? Watch this."

River didn't even try to guard her.

Kammie used the same underhanded shot. It hit the backboard—and dropped through the net.

"Nine to eight," Kammie sang out.

"Why didn't you guard her?" the coach asked.

River shrugged as Kammie faked left, then went right, and laid the ball in.

"*Woo hoo!* I win," Kammie announced loud enough for everyone in the gym to hear. "Eleven to eight." She tossed the ball up into the bleachers in celebration. Wilfred, who was still sitting there, screamed and ducked.

Coach Glover blew his whistle. "Never," he said to Kammie, "throw the ball away."

"The game was over! I won!"

"Never," he repeated, "throw the ball away. Three suicides. Everyone else hit the showers."

Coach Glover had said that attitude was as important as skills. River shook scaredy-cat Wilfred's hand and said, "Good luck!" She patted goof-off Erica's back and said, "Good luck!" When she told Jennifer, "Good luck," the other girl had a steely look in her eyes that was almost scary. Didn't she know that she could never make a team in a wheel-chair?

River even waited for Kammie to finish her suicides. She shook her hand and told her, "Good luck!"

3. THE HAUNTED MANSION

On Monday morning River stood in front of the team roster posted in the girls' locker room. Under the word *A-Team* was a list of eight girls. Under the word *B-Team* was everyone else who hadn't quit during try-outs, a list of six girls.

River Borowitz-Jacobs was the first name—on the B-Team.

As the crowd of girls pushed in around her, looking for their own names, River's skin turned ice cold. Their voices sounded as if they were coming from far away. She pushed through the group and sat down on a locker-room bench.

A mistake had been made. An accident. Her name was on the wrong list.

She heard Kammie's voice whoop, "All right! A-Team is gonna kick butt!" Then, "Hey! How come River's name isn't on here?"

Just shut up for once, River silently begged.

"There you are." Kammie plunked herself down on the bench next to her. "You didn't make the team," she shouted. "I don't get it. You're good. You're almost as good as me."

River jumped to her feet and left the locker room as fast as she could without running.

The rest of the day was a nightmare. The girls who made the A-Team, like Jeannie and Marianne and Sarah, and of course Kammie, were high-fiving, hanging out together at recess, already a tight clique. All morning River wanted to cry. Her chest felt like a big hollow basketball filled with too much air.

At three-fifteen, when the last bell rang, she ran to the gym where she found Coach Glover getting ready for the A-Team practice.

"Excuse me, but why didn't I make the team?"

"I'm sorry, young lady, but—"

"My name is River Borowitz-Jacobs."

He looked surprised at her interrupting.

"Look," he said. "I'm sorry I couldn't carry a bigger squad. You came close. But you don't have the height I need."

"I'm taller than Kammie Wilder."

"True. But she's an excellent ball handler. She's going to be my point guard. Besides, to be honest with you, I don't think you have the mental fortitude."

"What?"

"Uh . . . River?" he said as if he couldn't quite believe that was her name. She waited, and finally he went on. "I'm going to be frank with you. I need girls with killer instincts. Girls who are willing to stop at nothing, within the rules of course, to win. You're not an aggressive player, uh, River. You seemed more interested in fooling around. You didn't take the suicides seriously. You were more interested in trying trick shots than developing bread-and-butter skills. In your one-on-one game, you seemed to just give up. You have to want it, want it badly, to make a serious ball team."

So that explained why Kammie, who threw the ball into the bleachers, made the team and she didn't.

Coach Glover placed a hand on her shoulder and said, "But listen. Mrs. Sanders, Wilfred's mother, has agreed to coach the B-Team. So you'll get to play in the tournament."

Finding her voice, River said, "Mrs. Sanders has never played basketball in her life. You mean she is going to *baby-sit* the B-Team."

"Basketball is a metaphor for life," he said, turning away from her. "You win some, you lose some."

River didn't leave. Instead, she climbed to the top of the bleachers. From there, she watched the beginning of Coach Glover's first practice. He had picked the tallest girls, even if their skills weren't that good yet. And he had picked the girls who would mow down anyone in their paths to come in first. Every girl out there wanted to be MVP.

It was beginning to grow dark when River left the gym. And raining, of course, a soft drizzling rain with a bluster. She walked through town without even stopping under the Emily Hargraves banner. What was mental fortitude? Why didn't she have a killer instinct? Why, since she loved basketball so much, wasn't she on the A-Team?

When she came to the haunted house, River stopped to look at it from the road. Zack's friends had dared him to spend a night in it, and he was going to do it. Maybe in June, he'd said, when the weather cleared up. Robert and Carl would give him a hundred dollars if he did.

Back when Azalea was a booming logging town, the timber baron's house had been the fanciest in Azalea. People said that there was a huge ballroom inside where the timber baron had held lavish parties. Now the place was a wreck. Tall grasses and weeds surrounded the house. The white paint peeled off the wood siding like beech tree bark. Moss covered the roof and a couple of alder saplings had even taken root up there.

Even vandals stayed away. There were too many stories. Roger, Kammie's stepdad, said that when he was in high school, some kids had gone inside and never came out. He said that their dead bodies might still be in the house. But other people said that aliens lived inside. Zack's friend Robert claimed that he saw aliens take off in their spaceship in the field behind the house.

River decided to go in the house right then. No one would ever be able to say that she didn't have mental fortitude. Whatever that was.

River pushed through the tall grass. The rain had stopped and the wind stilled. Just above the house, a big moon broke out from behind the clouds.

Mental fortitude, she thought. Killer instinct.

She reached the front porch and slowly climbed the rickety wooden steps. She placed her hand on the cold doorknob. Before turning it, she let her gaze wander up the house. Tattered curtains hung in some of the windows. River half expected a hand to pull one aside, someone to gaze back down at her.

She tightened her grip and began turning the doorknob.

"What are you doing here?" a voice demanded.

River screamed. Her knees gave out and she fell onto the porch stairs. A hand grabbed hers and pulled her up.

4. KILLER INSTINCT

"What are you doing here, River?"

"Zack! You scared me. What are *you* doing here?"

"Talk about scared. I was walking home and I saw you out here, lurking in this creepy moonlight. Are you out of your mind? Why aren't you at practice, anyway? Wasn't today the first day?"

"I didn't make the team."

"*What?* No way."

River plopped down on the steps. "Coach Glover said I didn't have mental fortitude. He picked the tallest girls or the ones who were really aggressive."

Zack put his hands on his hips and stiffened his lips.

"It's the organic parents, isn't it?" she asked.

He nodded. "The nature name probably didn't help."

"I wish they'd named me Bullet."

"Yeah, or what would have been wrong with Susie?"

River looked at her brother to see if he was teasing. Secretly, she liked her name. He must have seen that he'd hurt her feelings, because he said, "I'm sorry about the team, River. But maybe we should get out of here."

River said, "The door's not locked."

"It's not?"

She shook her head. "Want to look inside?"

"No way. Are you crazy? I've got to go to practice. Come on, let's get off this porch."

"I thought you wanted to explore inside. I thought you were going to stay overnight in there."

"Yeah, sure, I *am* going to. But right now I have practice. Like in fifteen minutes. Now come on."

River slowly followed her brother, the bright moon beaming over their shoulders as they made their way back through the weeds.

When they reached the road, Zack said, "I'm sorry about the team. It's not fair. I'll see you later."

As Zack took off jogging down the road, River turned to look again at the haunted house. The word *B-Team* lodged in her throat like stale bread. But at least she would get to play in the tournament. There was still a chance that Emily Hargraves would scout her.

Then River thought of Kammie laughing with the other A-Team girls this morning. And Jeannie bragging about how her dad's hardware store was going to donate uniforms to the team. And how the A-Team already had a special handshake.

"It's not fair!" River yelled up at the dark sky.

A deep growl of thunder answered her. A minute later it was raining again. River looked one last time at the haunted house, then ran down the road to her own driveway.

At dinner that night River told her parents the news.

Her mom said, "I, for one, am happy you aren't playing for that man. Really, River, he's like an army sergeant." She cut a thick slice of lentil loaf, spooned some cracked wheat next to it, and passed the plate to Zack. "Soy milk or apple juice, honey?"

Zack held up the bottle of apple juice and read the label. "Vitamin enriched! This stuff is bad for you. I want pesticide-enriched juice."

"Mom, you don't understand," River persisted. "If I'm going to play for the WNBA, I need a coach like that. Coach Glover played for the New York Knicks. He's totally serious and tough."

"Tough! For goodness sakes, why do you have to be *tough*?"

Zack sighed and spoke slowly in the hopes that their parents would get it. "You can't become a good player unless you're tough."

"Oh, Zachary. Did I raise you to be tough?"

"No. That's why I'm having to work extra hard at it. That's exactly why I'm going to join the marines when I turn eighteen."

"Ohhh," their mom groaned.

"You're an artist, Mom," River said. "You don't understand anything."

"How exactly did 'artist' get to be a dirty word in our household?" Carolyn Borowitz asked her husband.

"If we wanted our kids to be artists," Larry Jacobs answered her, "we should have been professional athletes."

"Very funny," Zack said.

"I know you're disappointed, honey," River's mom said, "but think of all the time you'll have for doing other things."

Like what? What "other things" did she want to do? Her parents were clueless. They probably didn't even believe in mental fortitude.

"I know what we need!" her mom continued. "We need some sunshine. Let's ask the Sunny Day Goddess to make an appearance."

"Sure," Zack mumbled. "Why don't we say some affirmations, too."

"Will you please pass the bee pollen?" their dad asked.

River sighed and gave up.

After dinner her mom went out to her studio to check the work in her kiln. Her dad went into his darkroom to process the day's film. He must have put on one of his own CDs, because the songs of tropical birds floated out from under the darkroom door.

Zack knocked hard and called out, "Why can't we move to Hawaii if you like tropical birds so much?"

River flipped through her dad's CDs in the living room until she found the one of cascading avalanches. She put it on the player and turned it up full blast. Then she sunk into the beanbag chair and listened to the roar of rock and snow, over and over again.

The following afternoon River swung her gym bag onto the locker-room bench. As she began changing clothes for B-Team practice, the A-Team entered the locker room in one big pack.

Kammie chanted, "All the other teams had better *run,* because the Azalea A-Team is number *one!*"

Marianne whooped, "One, two three, *four,* Azalea A-Team is gonna score, score, *score!*"

Jeannie dropped a big plastic bag on the locker-room floor. She reached in and pulled out a pile of red and white T-shirts. "Practice jerseys," she said, handing them out. Each

A-Team player had one with her own name printed on the back.

River dressed quickly and stepped into the gym.

On one end of the court, Coach Glover was working with Rochelle on her free throw. On the other end, a bunch of little boys and girls were running around playing tag.

"Oh, River." Coach Glover took two long steps and stood before her. "I tried to talk the school into letting the B-Team use half the gym. But they need it for the after-school program. It was hard enough getting them to let me use half for the A-Team."

"Where is the B-Team practicing, then?" River hated even saying the word *B-Team*.

"I'm afraid you'll have to use the outside court." Coach Glover grimaced as if he cared. He patted River on the back. "I'm sorry I can't carry a bigger squad, kiddo."

River wriggled her shoulder out from under his big hand. Watching the A-Team girls run into the gym in their new practice jerseys made mental fortitude impossible.

She just wanted to go home and cry. But she didn't want him to see her give up. So she pushed open the door to the outside court.

It wasn't as if she hadn't played hoops outside a million times. It wasn't raining that hard. She had played basketball in worse weather than this. She started shooting baskets, wondering where the rest of the B-Team was.

First Wilfred and her mother, the coach, arrived. Then Jennifer rolled up with her fourth-grade sister, Megan, riding the back of the wheelchair. By four o'clock, no one else had shown up. There were five people, if you counted mothers and little sisters.

"Well, what can you expect in this weather?" asked Mrs. Sanders, who was huddled under the gym's overhang. As if there was ever any other kind of weather. She was actually wearing a wool skirt to coach in.

"I guess we might as well go home," River said.

"Why?" Jennifer asked. "We can still play two on two."

River counted again, in case she had missed someone. Herself. Wilfred. Jennifer.

That was three. Or did Jennifer mean to include Megan?

"Oh, dear," said Mrs. Sanders, "how many girls make a team?"

"Five, Mom," Wilfred said through gritted teeth.

"Oh, dear," Mrs. Sanders said again. "Well, I've got just the thing to get us started." She reached into the big bag at her feet and pulled out a Tupperware container of oatmeal cookies. After opening this and setting it down on the dry pavement under the building's overhang, she withdrew a big thermos from the bag. She poured out four cups of hot chocolate.

Cookies and cocoa. As if this were a sewing club and not a basketball team. The A-Team was probably running suicides already.

There was nothing to do but accept the cup of cocoa and huddle under the overhang. Wilfred slurped hers until Mrs. Sanders said, "Honey?" and shook her head gently at her daughter. Wilfred slurped louder.

"Thanks for the snacks," River told Mrs. Sanders. "I guess we better cancel practice."

"Because of my mom?" Wilfred asked, right in front of Mrs. Sanders.

"Um." River stalled, trying to think of what to say. "The cookies were great. Thanks. It's just that we don't have enough players for a team."

"Why are you giving up before we've even started?" Jennifer asked. "We can recruit more players."

"Sure, right." River looked at her wet sneakers.

Erica burst out of the gym door. She clicked off her cell phone, jammed it in a pocket, and said, "Why are you all eating? Don't we have practice?"

"This is all who showed up," Megan piped up as if she were a part of the team.

Erica lifted a finger and counted, pointing at River, Jennifer, Wilfred, and herself.

"Five," Megan said, punching a finger at her own chest. "You're gonna need me."

"This is a sixth-grade team," Jennifer said.

"A sixth-grade team with only four players, which is why you'll need me."

"I'm going home," River said. "I've got lots of homework." She turned and walked off without looking back.

But she didn't go home. Instead she went into the gym and climbed up the bleachers. The A-Team ran half a dozen suicides. They shot a hundred free throws each. They jumped rope for what seemed like hours. River watched all afternoon. Then she returned the next afternoon, sitting high up in the bleachers again. The A-Team spent that entire first week on conditioning and drills. They didn't play a minute of basketball.

That evening, after Coach Glover released the girls, he approached the bleachers and climbed up to her. Without saying a word, he sat down and looked out at the empty gym. The basketball looked the size of a grapefruit in his big hands.

"I heard you quit the B-Team," he finally said.

"I didn't quit," she replied, feeling her face get hot. "There *was* no B-Team. Only four girls showed up."

"This is your chance to show some leadership," he went on in a soft voice. "You could pull that team together. I'm sure of it."

The kindness in his voice jolted River. She looked at him quickly.

He placed the basketball in her hands and said, "What does that feel like to you?"

River almost laughed. "A basketball?"

"No, I mean in your heart."

When she didn't answer, he said, "Close your eyes and think."

So she did. Holding the basketball in her hands, River closed her eyes and thought. She felt the little nubbly bumps on the ball. She felt the intense pressure of air pushing out on the ball's skin. She felt the way the ball would roll off her fingers when she took a shot. She felt how it would fill her hands as she received a perfect pass. Like she was holding joy.

She opened her eyes and to her surprise, one word popped out. "Mine," she said.

Then embarrassed, in case he might think she meant the ball itself, she quickly handed it back to him. But somehow she thought he did understand her. He nodded. Then he stood and smiled. "Think about the B-Team, will you? I was counting on having them for the A-Team to scrimmage."

So that was it. He just wanted a practice squad for the A-Team.

He must have read the expression on her face, because he said, "Sure I'm thinking of my team, River. I'm always thinking of my team. You know why? I want that tournament title. Every suicide my girls run brings us that much closer. It's the small steps that count. The small steps toward your goal. If you give up before you've even taken the first step, how are you ever going to fly?"

With that, he stood to his full six feet eight inches, bending briefly to place the basketball back in her hands. Then he strode down the bleachers. River wished, now more than ever, that she was on the A-Team.

5. HOOP GIRLZ

By early Saturday morning River had decided. There was no way she was going to play for the B-Team.

But she *was* going to play in the Oregon Coast Tournament.

She told her mother, "I want to do an art project this weekend."

Carolyn Borowitz's face lit up. "What a good idea!"

"I'd like to silk-screen some T-shirts."

"What fun!" her mom said too enthusiastically. She whipped out a sketching pad and her pencil. "Let's design it right now."

"No problem." River explained exactly what she wanted: a spinning basketball hovering over a hoop and net. On the back of the T-shirt, her team's name.

Her mother's smile faded.

"It's my artistic vision, Mom," River said. "Here." She took the pencil out of her mom's hand and drew what she had in mind.

By Sunday night River had six purple—her favorite color—T-shirts. Even her mom admitted that the spinning basketball, hoop, and net looked "dynamic." River folded the T-shirts carefully and packed them in her knapsack.

On Monday morning she, Zack, and Kammie all dribbled basketballs as they walked to school. Kammie, of course, was chattering.

"We decided," she reported, "to just keep the name A-Team. You know, like *A* for *Azalea*. But also because of the letter *A*, the first letter, as in number one. First place."

Zack gave River a look that said, *If you want me to tell her to shut up, I will.*

River shrugged. It didn't really matter anymore. She had her own plans.

Zack changed the subject, anyway. "As soon as it's daylight savings again, I'm spending a night in the mansion and collecting my hundred bucks."

"The aliens will get you," Kammie said, dribbling the ball between her scissored legs.

River said, "I thought you were going to wait for summer. It would be totally creepy if there was a thunder and lightning storm while you were there."

"I could make them add another fifty dollars if there were thunder and lightning," Zack said thoughtfully. "Anyway, Robert and Carl said if I waited for summer, it would be just like camping. It wouldn't be a challenge."

"As if they'd ever spent a night there, in any season," River said. She tossed her basketball straight up toward the clouds, giving it a good spin.

"What's the big deal?" Kammie asked. "My stepbrother slept in there. Just last year. He did it for nothing. And there was a hurricane that night."

"No way," Zack said.

"Bets?"

"Then how come we never heard about it?" River asked.

"He's not a bragger."

"Oh, right," Zack said. "Real modest, just like you."

"I'm more modest than Rochelle," Kammie declared. "She's, like, so quiet. But I can tell that she thinks she's better than everyone. She never says anything, except to answer his questions. Well, duh, of course she knows the answers to his questions. He's her father. She just assumes she'll be MVP."

"If she's the best player, then she should be MVP," River said.

"She's not the best player. Her father might be the coach, but Emily Hargraves is choosing the MVP. And do you know who it's going to be?"

"Let me guess," Zack said. "You?"

"You got that right." Kammie tossed her basketball down the road, then chased after it. Grabbing the ball, she yelled, "Drive to the left, drive to the *right,* the A-Team girls have the meanest *bite.*" She dribbled in circles around each of her legs.

"At least," River mumbled to her brother, "I don't have to play on the same team as Kammie Wilder."

At school, River headed in the opposite direction of her homeroom.

"Where are you going?" Kammie asked.

Ignoring her, River marched into the girls' locker room, armed with a big fat purple magic marker. She raised it above the two team rosters and drew a line through the word *B-Team*. In its place, she wrote *Hoop Girlz*. Then she wrote a note announcing that her team would practice daily on the outside court. In big letters at the bottom of the sheet of paper, she wrote: *Goal: Fun.*

"You spelled 'girls' wrong," said Kammie, who had followed her.

"It's a statement of rebellion," River said.

That shut up Kammie for a moment. But then she asked, "What is Hoop Girlz?"

"*My* basketball team."

"Who're you gonna play?"

"We're entering the tournament."

"What about the B-Team?"

"What about them?" River shoved the purple magic marker into her front pocket like a gun in a holster.

Kammie's face went slack. She reached up

and twisted a strand of hair. For once, she had nothing to say.

"Come on," River said. "We're going to be late for class."

During the day, River spoke to all the girls who hadn't made the A-Team. But it was still raining at 3:00, so once again, only Wilfred, Erica, and Jennifer, with Megan in tow, showed up. River presented the purple T-shirts she had silk-screened and told them her plans for entering the tournament. She explained that she had watched the A-Team practice all last week, and that all they did were boring drills. She announced, "Hoop Girlz are gonna have fun."

"Hoop Girlz," Erica said happily, pulling on the new T-shirt. "I like that." She clicked on her cell phone. "Hey, Mom," she said after a minute, "you should see these T-shirts River made. They are so cool."

"Erica, get off the phone," Jennifer said, rolling her eyes at River. "Let's get started. Who's coaching?"

Megan cleared her throat loudly.

"Let's just play," River suggested.

"Okay," Jennifer agreed hesitantly, "but I want to practice our skills, too. It's possible we could beat the A-Team."

Not likely, River thought.

"What about my T-shirt?" Megan asked. "You're gonna need me."

There was no way around it. They would need Megan if no other sixth-grade girls joined the team. River reached into the bag and tossed Megan a T-shirt.

"Who's coaching?" Jennifer asked again.

"Not my mother!" Wilfred begged.

"Maybe we don't need a coach," River suggested uncertainly.

"Yeah," Megan agreed, now wearing her new T-shirt, which was so big on her it looked like a dress. "We just want to have fun. Right, River?"

"You can play," Jennifer said to her sister, "but you can't talk."

Megan's eyes became two blue lakes of tears.

"Maybe some layups first," River said to break the tension.

"Suicides!" Erica boomed out in a low voice, imitating Coach Glover.

River and Jennifer laughed, but Wilfred jogged over to the end line. She looked at the rest of them and said, "Well? We are going to play in the tournament, aren't we?"

River hesitated, then said, "Yeah."

"Then we have to practice." This time Wilfred did the imitation. "Suicides!" she boomed.

Erica placed two fingers to her mouth and produced a shrill whistle. "Hoop Girlz to the end line!" she called out.

"Go!" Jennifer yelled.

Wilfred might have been the world's biggest scaredy-cat, but she was fast. She beat River by about twenty yards.

Jennifer was the slowest, but when River tried to push her chair on the second suicide, Jennifer said, "Don't! You have to get strong legs. I have to get strong arms."

After running a couple of suicides, River said, "Let's play!"

"Yeah!" Erica sang out. "Hoop Girlz just want to have fun, fun, fun."

They played hard, until their purple T-shirts were soaked with sweat. Their hair flew out of their barrettes and elastic bands.

River's muscles felt so loose, it was as if she flowed through the air, bouncing effortlessly off the pavement. After every score, all five girls sang, "Hoop Girlz just wanna have fun, fun, fun."

Soon it grew dark. "I don't want to stop playing," Erica complained, "but I can hardly see."

Just then they were bathed in a splash of light. Someone had switched on the outside court lights.

"Wow," Jennifer said.

"It's the Basketball Court Goddess," River announced. Her mother always credited goddesses with small miracles.

They played and played and played until Jennifer finally said, "One more basket. Then we better go down to the parking lot. My dad is picking up me and Megan at 5:30."

River took a shot from the three-point line, heaving the basketball as hard as she could. It was a flat shot, soaring straight for the backboard. At least it won't be an air ball, she thought. It struck the backboard and ricocheted off the hoop. All five girls laughed and then raised their fists, singing, "Hoop Girlz just want to have fun, fun, fun."

"Hoop Girlz rule!" Jennifer cried.

Megan jumped on the back of her wheelchair and said, "Ride 'em, cowboy!"

Just then the A-Team burst out of the gym door.

"It's not fair," Marianne was complaining. "Everything centers on her."

"Get the ball to Rochelle! Get the ball to Rochelle!" Jeannie mimicked Coach Glover.

The A-Team girls suddenly stopped, all together, like a herd of animals. They had noticed the Hoop Girlz.

Jeannie snickered, "Look at their hippie uniforms. Tie dye!"

"It's silk screen," River corrected.

"Whatever. They're dorky."

"I think they're cute," Sarah said.

"They're going to enter the tournament," Kammie told her teammates.

"How could they?" said Marianne. "They only have three players."

The Hoop Girlz stood in a semicircle, all wearing their purple T-shirts. Five girls. But

Sarah had said *three*. River knew who she was counting—and who she wasn't counting. Everyone knew. The two teams stared at each other for a long, silent moment.

Suddenly Erica called out, "The A-Team had better run, run, *run*, because the Hoop Girlz have a lot more *fun*."

"What*ever*," Jeannie said again as the A-Team wandered off in a pack. "If they think that's a team, that's their problem."

Kammie, who stayed back to walk home with River, called out to the retreating backs of the A-Team girls. "See you tomorrow!"

River said good-bye to the other Hoop Girlz and asked Kammie, "Ready?"

"I want to show you something before we go," Kammie said. "Come look in the gym."

Curious, River followed Kammie inside.

Rochelle stood under one of the backboards, her long arms dangling at her sides. Her father was planted on the free-throw line, his hands on his hips. Another man, even taller than Coach Glover, stood next to Rochelle.

"Yank it out of the air," he told her, demonstrating a rebound. "Elbows out. Pull that ball down and protect it with your body."

Kammie nudged River and whispered, "Private rebounding lessons. Just for Rochelle. It's a friend of Coach Glover's from the NBA."

"Wow," River whispered.

"Yeah," Kammie said. "She has a private trainer, too."

"With all that help, she'll definitely get MVP."

"No, she won't," Kammie said.

6. THE KINGDOM OF BASKETBALL

"We need to practice our dribbling," Jennifer announced one day. "There are too many turnovers."

"What's a turnover?" Megan asked.

"Fried crispy on the outside, hot apples on the inside," Erica said.

"Jennifer's right," River said. "My left hand dribble is weak."

So the girls practiced dribbling, three minutes with each hand.

"I do this at home," Jennifer said. "We all should."

"I do this at home," Erica started to mimic Jennifer.

"What you need to practice," River interrupted her, "is your rebounding. You're tall.

You could get a lot of rebounds if you concentrated on getting in position."

River told them what the private coach had told Rochelle. Use your body to block out other players. Hold your elbows out so you take up lots of space. Yank the ball out of the air.

For the next half an hour, the girls had Megan toss the ball against the backboard. They took turns jumping for the rebounds.

"Now we should add a defense player," Jennifer said.

River and the other girls stared at her. Sometimes it was as if Jennifer didn't even know she was in a wheelchair. With a defensive player, there was no way she could get a rebound.

"Erica," Jennifer said. "You defend me."

Erica shrugged. The two girls moved under the basket. Megan tossed the ball against the backboard. Jennifer bent forward and hurled toward it. Her chair hit Erica in the shins. Erica shrieked and jumped aside. Jennifer snatched the rebound.

As Erica hopped around, saying, "Ouch, ouch, ouch," Jennifer sat with the ball in her lap, staring at the rest of the girls with a ferocity in her eyes.

River cracked up.

All the girls laughed then, but they ran a lot more drills that day. In fact, the less they goofed off, the more fun River had. Not only did they practice their dribbling and rebounding, they worked on passing and shooting free throws.

That afternoon River felt as if she charged right through a door into a magical place. Basketball became its own kingdom. She didn't feel the cold air slapping her sweaty face. She didn't feel her tired muscles. Her body became pure movement. Pure joy.

The magic wasn't just inside her, though. Every evening the lights came on around dusk. The girls all sang out, "Basketball Court Goddess!" but River was puzzled. She'd thought the lights were on a timer and came on automatically. But later she noticed they didn't always come on at the exact same time.

Then there was the day it rained so hard she knew the outside court would be swamped, even though the rain stopped by two o'clock. But when she checked the court after school, someone had swept all the puddles away.

"The Basketball Court Goddess," she whispered, looking over both shoulders.

The other girls didn't seem to even notice. Jennifer called out, "Rebounding drills!" and they got to work.

That was the moment River started to believe again. It was possible that the Hoop Girlz could win. It was possible that Emily Hargraves could name River MVP. In the magical kingdom of basketball, a lot was possible. River started dribbling with her left hand for ten full minutes every day. She shot one hundred free throws every day. If only they could find another team to scrimmage.

One evening, just a week and a half before the tournament, River's mom swung by the school on her way home from town to give River and Kammie a ride. She invited Kammie in for dinner and, of course, Kammie said yes.

"What's this?" Kammie asked, shoveling

in a mouthful before anyone else had even pulled out their napkins. "Meatballs and gravy?" She grinned as she chomped down on her big bite. Then, "Achhh! Ach! Ach!" She spit out the grayish lump. "Gross."

Carolyn Borowitz's and Larry Jacobs's eyes met across the table. Carolyn only said, "Kammie, dear, that's not polite." As usual, Kammie got away with murder.

"Fine," Kammie said, "but the point is, what *is* this?"

River rolled her eyes at her brother.

"It's braised tofu," Carolyn Jacobs said firmly. "On brown rice."

"And this?" Kammie asked, jabbing her fork at another pile on her plate.

"Black-eyed peas."

"Whew. Nasty looking. But I'll give it another go."

Kammie started eating, shoveling in forkful after forkful, and cleaned her plate up in no time.

That didn't stop her from talking, though. First, she filled in the Borowitz-Jacobs family on what was happening with the A-Team.

Each of the girls on the team thought she should win the title of MVP. They were all mad at the coach for favoring Rochelle.

"I've got it sewn up, though," Kammie concluded. "Unless Coach Glover pays off Emily Hargraves or something. Roger told me that kind of thing does happen. But I don't think Emily would go for it. She'll see who's the best basketball player. Hah!" Kammie laughed and jumped up to get more juice from the fridge.

Of course tonight, with Kammie talking, River's mom took a big interest in basketball. She listened to everything Kammie said, asked questions, and acted like Kammie was the next star of the WNBA.

When she could get a word in edgewise, River said, "You know, Mom. You were right. It's stupid to take basketball that seriously."

Zack scowled at her. "What are you talking about?"

"Hoop Girlz just want to have fun," she said, trying to sound casual.

"Oh, right," Zack said. "That's just because you don't have a chance of being MVP."

"It is not."

"It is, too."

"Never mind," her mother said as if they were arguing about something as insignificant as Tinkertoys. "More braised tofu, honey?"

"I'll have some!" Kammie reached her plate toward Carolyn Borowitz.

"I thought you didn't like it," River said.

"Just had to get used to it. Besides, after those practices of Coach Glover's, I'd eat anything. But hold the black-eyes. Can't stomach them."

"Black-eyed peas," Zack corrected.

"Whatever," Kammie said, and began shoveling in food again.

Later that night, after Kammie had gone home, Zack poked his head into River's room. "Coach Glover was right," he said. "You don't have what it takes."

River worked out a math problem, ignoring him, pretending like she didn't care what he thought. He was just mad about what she had said at dinner.

"Next thing I know, you'll take up knitting or . . . or . . ." Zack struggled to think of something worse. "Or jump rope."

River turned the page of her math book and looked at the next set of problems.

Zack tried a different tack. "You're a better ball player than half the girls on the A-Team."

It worked. River couldn't help looking up. "What do you mean?"

"I've watched the A-Team practice."

"You have?"

"I watched two practices of theirs this week. Sure, they have height. Some talent, too. But Coach Glover is banking everything on Rochelle. All you'd have to do is double-team her."

"What's that mean?"

"Put two defensive players on her. She'd have a much harder time getting the ball. Or doing anything with it when she did."

"But that would leave a player open."

"Yeah, but if the team has spent all its time setting up Rochelle, that open player might not be ready to do much with the ball."

River got that kingdom of basketball feeling again. Power in her fingertips. Roaring in her ears.

"But," she said, "we have only four players,

unless you count Megan, Jennifer's fourth-grade sister."

"What kind of skills does your team have?"

River described the Hoop Girlz's strengths and weaknesses.

"Jennifer has a good shot?"

"A great shot. But like, in her chair, she's only about three feet tall. In a real game, she'd never get her shot off."

"That's easy."

"It is?"

"Sure. You just need to run a play. Set a pick on the player who is guarding Jennifer. She only needs a second to get her shot off, right?"

River nodded.

"I guess I could show you a couple of plays," Zack said. "My own team practice doesn't start until five o'clock."

River slammed her math book shut. "Really?"

"Yeah, I guess I could."

"Tomorrow?"

"When is the tournament?"

"In a week and a half."

"Okay. I'll come by your practice tomorrow."

River jumped up from her desk, pushing past Zack. "Mom?" she called down the stairs. "I changed my mind again. Basketball *is* the most important thing in the world."

The next day Zack arrived at the Hoop Girlz practice with a whistle and a fat piece of chalk.

"Two on two," he announced before River even had a chance to introduce him. "Jennifer and Erica against River and Wilfred. I need to assess your skills."

"This is my brother," River said apologetically, thinking that maybe this was a big mistake. "He's going to show us some ways to play against the A-Team."

"He looks like Coach Glover with that whistle in his mouth," Wilfred complained.

"He can only coach us if he wears a T-shirt that says *Hoop Girlz*," Erica giggled.

"Just be quiet and listen to what he says," Jennifer advised with a scowl.

What a big mistake, River thought.

But as soon as they started to play, River forgot all about her brother being there. She sunk her first shot, high-fived Wilfred, and took the ball to the top of the key. River faked a jumper and fired the ball to Wilfred. Unfortunately, her fake fooled Wilfred as well as the defense. The ball glanced off her shoulder. Wilfred yowled.

"Oh! Sorry!" River said.

A shrill whistle brought her out of the game. All the girls looked at Zack.

"Sorry," River said.

"Never," Zack said in a voice deeper than his usual one, "say 'sorry' on the basketball court."

"But I hit Wilfred with the ball!"

"That was a good fake and pass. Wilfred is the one who messed up."

"He's just like Coach Glover," Wilfred complained again. "He's just siding with his sister."

"The point is," Zack said with an exaggerated sigh, "that athletes never apologize on the court. It doesn't matter who is at fault. Basketball is a physical game."

"Yeah," Jennifer agreed. "You have to be aggressive. Zack is right."

"Okay," Zack said. "Resume play."

The girls all stared at him.

Finally, Wilfred said, "How do you 'resume'?"

"That means start playing again," Jennifer said with exasperation.

After another couple of points, River got the ball. As she started for the basket, Jennifer flew in to guard her. Her wheelchair rammed River in the shins.

"Ow!" River cried.

"Sorry," Jennifer said.

River rubbed the red welt that was already forming on her shin.

"Hey!" Zack called out. "What did I just tell River?"

"Whoops. Sorry," Jennifer said. "I didn't mean to say 'sorry.'"

The Hoop Girlz all laughed.

Zack blew his whistle.

In his deep coach-voice, he demanded, "Do you want me to coach or not?"

"Yes, yes!" they all called out, still giggling. Then they all said, "Sorry!" and started laughing all over again.

"Suicides!" Zack ordered as punishment.

The girls hustled to the end line. Zack looked surprised they knew what suicides were. When he blew his whistle, they took off.

"Okay," Zack said, obviously impressed. "You've got some potential. Here's my plan."

This time the shrill sound wasn't Zack's whistle. It was Erica's cell phone.

"Just a sec," she said, running off the court. "Hello?" Then, "Hey!" when Zack plucked the phone out of her hand and punched the off button.

"That was my mom you hung up on!"

"Your mom will be there when you get home." Zack shoved the phone in his back pocket.

"He *is* just like Coach Glover," Wilfred whined. She folded her arms across her chest and backed up a couple of steps, as if Zack were a big bull about to charge her.

"Get a grip, Wilfred," Jennifer said sternly. "He's just being realistic. We can't be wimps on the court. We need to find ways to use our skills. You need to quit being so scared. River needs to quit being so nice. Erica needs to leave her phone alone. What about me, Zack?"

"I have plans for you," he told her.

"You do?" Jennifer had expected Zack to falter on that question. She rolled closer to him.

"Everyone gather around," he said, picking up his fat piece of chalk. "Play number one."

Zack drew a diagram on the pavement. He showed how Jennifer was to get in the corner of the key, her favorite place to shoot. Then Erica was to set a pick, meaning block the player defending Jennifer. Erica had to plant herself solidly so that it would be difficult for the player to get around her. Then Jennifer had to wheel around the two players—as quickly as she could—and take her shot. She would have only a second.

"Have I made myself clear?" Zack asked.

"Yes, sir!" the girls sang out.

River laughed at her brother's new coach personality, but Jennifer's eyes were gleaming. She was the first one on the court to try out the new play. They needed to use Megan, so they would have five offensive players. Since there were no defensive players, Zack defended Jennifer. Erica set the pick on him. It worked! Jennifer popped in her shot.

Then they ran the play over and over again, about fifty times.

"It's called muscle memory," Zack said. "You have to get so you know what to do without thinking."

Next, he showed the Hoop Girlz a fast-break play that would use Wilfred's speed. "The second you get a rebound," he said, "Wilfred takes off for the basket. Full speed, got it?" Wilfred nodded. "Then, Erica, I think you have the strongest arm. You hurl the ball down to her. With Wilfred's speed, she should be all alone under your basket. You catch the ball and do a simple layup, okay?"

"That's too much pressure!" Wilfred said. "I can't shoot under pressure."

"Get used to it," Jennifer advised.

"You'll be all alone under the basket," Erica said. "There won't be any defensive players nearby."

"But you'll all be counting on me."

"That's the whole point," Zack growled. "That's what we're doing here. The A-Team has some skills and a lot of height. But they don't have any teamwork. They have bad morale. The only way to beat them is by being smart. You have to count on one another."

Zack met eyes with each of the girls to make sure they understood. He held Wilfred's gaze. She practically trembled.

"You can do it," River whispered to her as they set up on the court.

Unfortunately, it didn't look as if she *could* do it. The first time the long pass came her way, Wilfred screamed and ducked. The ball flew off the court, down the hill, and rolled onto the soccer field. The second time, Erica threw the ball much more gently. It bounced in front of Wilfred. But Wilfred still dove to the side of the court, as if it were a bullet coming her way. The third time, Erica rolled the ball toward Wilfred. She managed to pick it up. But she couldn't make the layup. She tried four times.

"Wilfred," Jennifer scolded. "You make layups all the time. You're good at them."

"I know," Wilfred whimpered. "But the pressure."

"Excuse me," Erica said, "but *what* pressure? We are all standing on the far side of the court. No one is guarding you."

"Speaking of which," River said, "we need to find someone to scrimmage, don't we?"

Zack shook his head. "That would be good, but who . . . ?"

"*Find* someone," Jennifer said.

"I'll think about it. That's it for today." Zack used his sneaker to rub out the chalk play diagrams on the pavement.

"Hoop Girlz plays are top secret," Erica declared, clearly pleased with Zack.

Wilfred glared at him for a long time before racing off to catch her ride.

Jennifer, however, was so excited about the play he had made for her that she wheeled over to hug him. Embarrassed, Zack backed up. But Jennifer kept coming, accidentally ramming into *his* shins.

"Ouch!" he called out as she wrapped her arms around his legs and hugged.

"I'm *not* sorry," Jennifer said.

"Okay, okay," Zack said, pulling away from her. "I've got to get to my practice."

River was proud of her coach brother, even if he did use a fake voice. Even if he did act sort of like Coach Glover. The other Hoop Girlz liked him, except for maybe Wilfred, and that's what counted.

"You're right," Zack told River, using his regular voice once they were alone, "we have to find some defensive players for you to run the plays against."

"We have only a few days."

"I know," Zack said, thinking. "We'll have to be smart, come up with a good game plan for the tournament."

"You're coming to the tournament?"

"I'm the coach, aren't I?"

"Do you think we have a chance?"

"If you work very hard."

River spread her fingers around her basketball and closed her eyes. She heard the cheering fans. She smelled the varnished floors. She felt the ball roll expertly off her fingers. She saw the net sway gently back and forth after the ball fell through. An entire kingdom, right there between her fingertips and the orange ball.

7. COACH GLOVER'S OFFER

Zack coached the Hoop Girlz two more after-noons, but on Friday morning, a storm blew in. This storm was no Oregon coast drizzle, it was a full-blown hurricane washing in from the Pacific. Oceans of water sloshed through Azalea. The wind blew so hard, shingles ripped off the roof of the haunted mansion.

At lunchtime, River checked the outside basketball court. It was completely flooded. More water than the Basketball Court God-dess could sweep away. Besides, it was still raining. Even worse, the forecast was for more of the same for at least a week.

The tournament was next weekend. They had a coach. They had plays. And now they wouldn't be able to practice.

On Friday afternoon, after canceling practice, River sat in the warm, dry gym and watched the A-Team scrimmage with the junior high team. Then she walked home, keeping her head down against the rain and wind.

The Emily Hargraves banner had twisted in the wind. Rain filled the folds, causing the whole thing to sag. River stood directly under it, anyway, and, since everyone was indoors where they couldn't hear her, yelled, "Basketball Court Goddess! Help me find a place for my team to practice!"

Then she said her regular affirmation about making it to the WNBA some day.

When River got home, she changed into dry clothes, then threw herself into the beanbag chair to watch the rain. In frustration, she kicked the beanbag chair with her heels, accidentally knocking the phone sitting on the floor. The receiver fell out of its cradle and the dial tone buzzed. River pushed herself up and grabbed the Yellow Pages.

She called the community center. That gym was booked solid. So was the high school gym. So were all the gyms in neighboring towns. She even tried a private athletic club. Members only, and, anyway, the gym was booked for the week.

Finally, she called the school secretary, Mrs. Sawyer, to find out if maybe they could use the cafeteria. The answer was no.

"Liability," Mrs. Sawyer said.

"What does that mean?"

"If someone got hurt they could sue."

That evening, the phone rang during dinner. "I'll get it," River said. It would be Kammie. She liked coming over on Friday nights because the Borowitz-Jacobs always ate popcorn and watched videos.

River picked up the receiver and said, "Hoop Girlz rule. The A-Team sucks."

"River!" her mom called from the dinner table.

There was a long silence on the other end of the line.

Then, finally, a deep voice said, "This is Coach Glover. May I speak with River, please?"

A flush spread from a place behind River's eyes, across her whole face. She pulled the phone down from her ear and covered the mouthpiece with her hand. She waited a moment, as if she were River's sister running to get her, and then said, "Hello?"

Coach Glover said, "I have an idea I'd like to discuss with you."

"Yeah?" she said, remembering how in practice the girls were supposed to say, "Yes, sir."

"It's going to rain the rest of this week. Your team isn't going to be able to practice outside."

She knew what he wanted: another team for the A-Team to scrimmage. As much as she'd like to play indoors, she wasn't about to let him see their plays.

"We'll be fine." River said. "The rain is okay."

"The reason I called," Coach Glover continued, "is because I'd like to invite you to play for the A-Team."

"The A-Team?"

"Yes."

"Me?"

"If I'm speaking to River Borowitz-Jacobs."

"Yes, sir," River said. "That's me."

"I've admired your initiative in pulling together the B-Team—"

"Hoop Girlz."

"Pardon me?"

"My team is called Hoop Girlz, not the B-Team."

"Yes, well. My point is, I believe you could contribute to the A-Team. I'm afraid the weather is going to prevent use of the outside court the rest of the week. I wanted to give you a chance to play in the tournament."

A place on the A-Team!

River whispered, "Yes, sir."

"So," Coach Glover continued, "we'll see you in the gym on Monday afternoon, 3:30 sharp. I'll have a practice jersey made up for you. See you then."

He hung up and River shouted, "Yes, sir!"

The A-Team. A jersey with her name on it. This was her chance. Now Emily Hargraves would scout her for sure. How was she ever going to be able to wait until Monday afternoon at 3:30? It was only 7:00 Friday evening.

River slipped into her seat at the dinner table. She knew her mother wouldn't be too pleased about the promotion to the A-Team. Now that Zack was the Hoop Girlz coach, he probably wouldn't take the news too enthusiastically, either. She kept quiet for the time being.

"That's going to be a lot of work," her dad was saying.

"What?" River asked, thinking they'd heard Coach Glover's offer.

"Someone bought the haunted mansion," Zack said.

"They're going to fix it up and live there," her mother added.

Zack asked, "Do you think that place is really haunted?"

Their mom said, "Of course not. But I wouldn't want to go inside."

"Why not?" Zack asked, his voice cracking.

"Rodents."

"You think there are rodents in there?"

"I wouldn't doubt it."

"Like rats?"

"Rats, mice, all sorts of vermin."

"What about aliens?" River asked.

"It's my understanding," her mother said dryly, "that aliens live in outer space, not in run-down houses here on Earth."

After dinner the phone rang again. Zack answered and took the phone into his bedroom. He talked in a low voice for a long time.

River volunteered to do the dishes. Then she watched a video with her family, but she was so excited that she could hardly sit still. When she went to bed, she couldn't sleep. All she could think about was playing for the WNBA, maybe with the Portland Storm or the Los Angeles Sparks or even the Houston Comets. Now that she was on the A-Team, all she had to do was play well in the tournament. Emily Hargraves would help her with the rest.

At midnight there was a soft tap at her door. Zack slipped in and shut it behind him. "Shh," he said before she even spoke. "Want to help me with something?"

"What?"

"You heard Dad saying that someone's bought the haunted mansion. That means I've got to carry out my mission now. Robert and Carl said they'd double the payoff—making it two hundred dollars—if I slept there tonight. In the storm."

"You're crazy."

"I'm going to do it, but I need proof. I

would take my Polaroid, but it's broken. You have to come with me. That way I'll have a witness that I actually did it."

"Come with you and sleep in the haunted mansion," River said in a flat voice. "Are you kidding?"

"I helped with the Hoop Girlz when you needed me."

True. But coaching a basketball team wasn't exactly the same thing as staying overnight in a haunted mansion.

"Mom and Dad will kill you."

"They won't know we did it. We leave now. We're back in the house by five-thirty. So it's basically a five-hour commitment. Piece of cake."

When River was silent, Zack said, "You don't do this, I'll quit coaching the Hoop Girlz."

River should have said, "Fine!" On Monday, she started playing for the A-Team, anyway. Somehow, though, his threat made her feel bad.

Zack misinterpreted her silence. He said, "Okay, this is my final offer. I'll give you fifty dollars of the payoff. That's entirely fair because I'm the one who made the deal. And I've packed all our gear. See? I have a rain poncho and snacks for you, right here."

Add that fifty dollars to her savings, and she might have enough money to buy sneakers like Emily Hargraves's for the tournament.

"I'm in," she said.

8. THE BALLROOM

River and Zack each wore a green rain poncho. Under his, Zack wore a backpack into which he had stuffed two sleeping bags, an alarm clock, and his entire stash of contraband snacks, including candy bars, pepperoni sticks, and a big bag of barbecue potato chips. River had a flashlight and Zack brought the Coleman lantern.

The rain still pelted down. The ditches on either side of the road were gushing rivers. The dark clouds hung thick and low, blocking out even the idea of starlight.

As they walked down the road, Zack's pace slowed. "I'm going to light the lantern."

"You can't," River said. "Someone might see us."

As they started up the overgrown driveway of the timber baron's house, Zack used his deep coach voice to insist, "We need light now."

"Save the lantern for inside." River switched on her flashlight.

"This is stupid," Zack said when they reached the front porch.

"Then go home." River grasped the brass doorknob.

"Yeah, and leave my baby sister to be carried off by aliens?" He stomped up the stairs, as if making lots of noise would scare off any ghosts or aliens inside.

Though the knob turned easily, the door wouldn't open. River threw her hip against it and pushed.

"Locked," Zack concluded. "Let's go."

River pulled back, then threw her hip against the door with more force. The door opened.

"Anyone home?" River called out.

"Shh," Zack hissed.

"Why?" she asked. "Do you think they're sleeping?"

"Very funny."

The large entry room smelled wet and moldy. Near the back was a wide stairway, leading to the second floor. River crept across the entry to an open door on the right. Shining her flashlight, she saw a huge room with a wooden floor, high ceilings, and the remains of two crystal chandeliers. The ballroom.

"Turn on the lantern," she said. "So we can see better."

She held the beam of her flashlight on the lantern while Zack lit a match and then the lantern. A quavering pool of light splashed across the floor.

"Wow," River said as Zack swung the lantern around. "This is enormous! It's practically as big as a basketball court."

Red wallpaper peeled off the walls. Spider silk filled in the missing parts of the chandeliers. In the corner sat a smashed grand piano, and along one of the walls, there were two sofas with wooden arms that looked like cat paws. Generations of mice, or worse, had made their homes in the stuffing.

The rain fell in sheets, making the ballroom

windows big smears of water. It was dry inside, though.

River pulled off her rain poncho. "We going to sleep in here?"

Zack made no move to take off his own poncho. He stayed right by the door of the ballroom, one hand grasping the knob and the other his lantern. The light played on his face, making *him* look like an alien.

"We're in," River said. "That was the scary part. See? No ghosts. No dead bodies. No aliens. All we have to do is spread out the sleeping bags and go to sleep. I think it's nicer here than in that entry."

"I can't believe you're not afraid," Zack said in a low gurgly voice. Then he swung his lantern wildly, lighting the far corner, under the grand piano. In a shout-whisper, he said, "What's that?"

River had seen something, too. Vermin, she thought. Rats, mice.

"Shut the door," she told her brother. "Before we know it, the night will be over. You'll be a hundred and fifty dollars richer. I'll have new sneakers for the tournament."

"So that's why you agreed to do this?"

She looked down at the worn ballroom floor, glad she hadn't blurted out anything about the A-Team. She would have to tell him, but not tonight.

Zack sloughed off the poncho and backpack. He yanked out the two sleeping bags and kicked one toward River. He set the alarm clock for five o'clock so that they could sneak back home before their parents awakened. Then they crawled into the sleeping bags.

"What now?" River asked.

"I'm eating." Zack opened the potato chips. When he bit into one, the crackle was so loud, they both flinched.

"Do you think there's anything up those stairs?" River asked.

Zack ate a candy bar in two bites and opened another one. "Don't talk about it."

"But if there is something up there, don't you want to know about it? Before we go to sleep?"

"Thanks a lot, River. Why did you have to say that? We could have just ignored the upstairs. But now you had to go and talk about it."

"I'll watch our stuff," River said. "You go have a look."

"No way. If you want your fifty bucks for new sneakers, you're coming, too."

Zack pushed off his sleeping bag and stood up. "Come on. We're checking out upstairs before we go to sleep."

They tiptoed out of the ballroom and stopped in the entry. "Up we go," Zack said. The stair boards creaked, of course. On one step River felt something squish under her foot. She didn't shine the flashlight on whatever it was. She didn't want to know.

When they reached the top of the spiral staircase, Zack said, "Ladies first."

"You're the oldest!"

"It was your idea to check out the upstairs!"

"What was that?" Zack dropped to all fours on the stairs.

"I didn't hear anything."

"I heard something like bedsprings. A long squeak."

"It's just the storm." River grabbed the

lantern out of Zack's hands and crested the stairs. "Oh, creepy!" she cried out.

"Give me a light!" Zack demanded. "You have both the flashlight and the lantern."

Shattered glass covered the upstairs hallway floor. A couple of old picture frames lay among the glass shards. One held a faded picture of an old lady wearing a bun and a white lace collar. Another torn photo showed a rigid young man with greased hair and a sour expression.

There were three closed doors in the hallway.

"Don't," Zack warned. "Just leave the doors alone."

"Robert and Carl are going to make you describe what you saw. Do you want to admit that you were afraid to open all the doors? Besides it's scarier *not* knowing what's behind these doors. I'll never get to sleep if we don't look." River reached for the first door and opened it.

A few beer bottles were scattered on the floor along with one doll's head. In the corner, there was a rocking horse.

"That rocking horse!" Zack said, his voice a whinny.

"What?"

"It's moving!"

"It is not!" The more scared Zack got, the less scared River felt. She jumped on the horse and rocked for a moment. "Why do you think the family left all their stuff here?" she asked. "Do you think maybe they all died of the plague or something?"

"Why don't I have a regular family?" Zack moaned. "A regular dad who drives a truck. A regular mom who serves milk and hamburgers for dinner. A regular little sister who screams when she sees a bug. Why isn't it like that?"

River pushed her brother out of the child's room, back into the hallway. "It's just old junk," she told him. "You don't have to be so scared. But okay, I won't open any more doors. I'm tired. Let's go to sleep."

"Finally, a sensible idea. We have to get up at five. Which is in about four hours."

They descended the spiral staircase and, once again, crawled into the sleeping bags on the ballroom floor. But they didn't fall asleep. They lay in the dark and listened to the rain pelt the windows. The wind howled across the fields. Sometimes an extra strong gust blew a tree branch against the side of the house, making a long scraping sound.

"At least there's no thunder and lightning," River said.

"Just be quiet," Zack said angrily.

So she was quiet for a couple of minutes. Then Zack said, "*Say* something. Talk!"

"Well, which do you want?"

"What's that?" Zack asked, sitting up suddenly.

"What?"

"I heard something again."

"Probably just the vermin."

"No, something outside."

"The wind."

"No, a different kind of sound! A clunking."

Zack was right. There it was. A clunking. On the front porch. Something pounded against the front door. Then the sound of the front door flying open and banging against the wall. Footsteps in the entry room.

"Quick, where's my flashlight?" River asked in a panic.

"It's too late," Zack quacked. "It's coming in."

A burst of light blinded River.

9. NO ESCAPE

"This isn't funny. It's not funny at all." Zack stood doubled over, his hands on his knees, catching his breath. River still lay in her sleeping bag. Her heart pounded so hard it felt as if it were pounding against the ballroom floorboards.

"Hey," said Robert. "How were we supposed to know you really did it if we didn't come see for ourselves?" He held his flashlight under his chin and made a ghoul face.

"Yeah, man," Carl said. "We had to check."

"You have to double the offer *again*," Zack said, lighting the lantern. "You owe me four hundred dollars."

"You didn't tell us you were bringing your

little sister as a bodyguard. You get exactly zero dollars. You cheated."

"I brought her as a witness! I knew you guys wouldn't believe I'd done it."

"Sorry, deal's off. No one agreed to little sisters." Carl scrambled over to the ancient grand piano. He hit a couple of keys. "Man, this place is weird."

"No one ever said alone," Zack said. "No one said I had to sleep here alone. Just that I had to spend a night. Besides, how could River be any help?"

Carl hit a few more keys of the silent piano. "This thing needs some tuning up."

River finally found her voice and said, "If you guys think you're so great, why don't you spend the night, too? There are a couple of spare rooms upstairs."

"Whoa. No way," Carl said, jumping away from the piano. "I'm outta here now."

"If you don't pay my brother, I'll tell your parents you snuck out in the night."

Zack said, "River is going through a blackmail stage."

"Don't worry," Robert said to River. "We'll

pay him. If he makes it through the night, that is. As for myself, I wouldn't spend another five minutes in this place. Come on, Carl. Let's get out of here. It's creepy."

The two boys turned toward the door, ready to leave.

"What's that?" Carl asked.

The window facing the highway turned into a bright rain-washed blur.

"It's like headlights," Robert said. "Who the . . . ? I didn't think a car could make it up that driveway. It's totally overgrown."

"Those are definitely headlights," Carl said. "But if they're not car headlights . . . Oh, man." Carl looked around frantically. He ran to the spiral staircase. "What's up here?" he demanded in a high squeaky voice. "What's up here? Come on, you guys, let's get upstairs! Quick! Before it gets here!"

River and Zack didn't answer. They watched the approaching glare. The lights were accompanied by a roar, like some kind of engine. Then the engine was cut. Whatever it was, it had stopped right in front of the house.

Robert and Carl were frantic, running to

the back of the house, searching for another way out. River knew there was no escape, so she stayed right where she was.

The front door opened.

Carl bleated.

Robert squealed, "Who is it?"

The intruder stomped through the entry room and stood in the doorway to the ballroom.

In the lantern light, River saw a fat man in a tan uniform, his hand resting on the butt of the gun in his holster. A voice bellowed, "This is the sheriff. Nobody move."

River couldn't have moved if she had wanted to. The sheriff slowly assessed the situation. He gradually let go of his gun and said again, "All of you remain exactly where you are."

First he frisked Zack, who was standing on top of his sleeping bag. Next he approached Carl and Robert at the bottom of the stairs. They looked terrified as he searched them. Robert squeaked, "We don't have anything illegal."

Finally the sheriff crouched down next to

River who was still sitting in her sleeping bag. "What's your name, young lady?"

"River Borowitz-Jacobs."

"River Borowitz-Jacobs? You're kidding."

River wished she were kidding. She shook her head slowly.

"Why, you're the girl who organized the Hoop Girlz, aren't you?"

She nodded.

"Is one of these boys your brother?"

River pointed at Zack.

The sheriff actually reached out and shook Zack's hand. "And you're the coach?" Suddenly a big smile spread across his face. "You're the boy who figured out that play for my Jennie."

"You're Jennifer's dad?" Zack asked.

"I sure am." He kept smiling, as if they had just met in a grocery store rather than in a haunted mansion in the middle of the night. Then he remembered his job and the smile faded. "Look, I got a call from a guy who was driving by this place and saw lights. What in the world are you kids up to?"

Zack, Carl, and Robert were still speechless. So River explained about her brother's bet.

The sheriff shook his head slowly. He sighed and said, "Come on. I'll run you all home. I'll have to speak to your parents. It's past curfew and this is private property."

Zack stuffed the sleeping bags into his backpack, and the four kids followed the sheriff out to his four-wheel drive truck. The vehicle plowed right through the weeds and back to the highway.

Carolyn Borowitz and Larry Jacobs were not amused when they opened the door at two in the morning to find their son and daughter, along with the sheriff, on the doorstep. Both kids were immediately grounded from all activities except school-related ones.

A few hours later, as the family ate breakfast, Zack said, "Basketball practice is school related, right? It's the school team."

"I suppose so," Carolyn Borowitz sighed. "But, River, I want you to come directly home after school on Monday."

"I have basketball practice, too!"

"Oh, no. No more basketball for you."

"That's sexist! You're saying that Zack's basketball team is more important than mine!"

Their parents looked at each other. Neither of them could tolerate being called sexist.

"Yeah," Zack said, sticking up for River. "In fact, it's extra sexist because River created Hoop Girlz. Just because it isn't an official school team doesn't make it less important."

This was River's chance to tell her family about the A-Team, but she couldn't get the words out. What was important right now was that she showed up for the A-Team practice on Monday.

"They have a point," their father said.

"If I had my way right now," their mother said, "I'd pack up your bags and send you both to live in the timber baron's mansion."

"So I can go to my basketball practice?" River asked.

"I have to go to the Hoop Girlz practice, too, because I'm coach," Zack put in.

"Fine," their mother said through tight lips. "And then straight home. You haven't heard the end of this. The sheriff, for Pete's sake."

10. THE DECISION

It rained hard the rest of the weekend. About ten times River started to tell Zack about being drafted up to the A-Team. This was her ticket to the WNBA. He would understand.

Why, then, every time she said, "Hey, Zack?" did she finish the sentence with something entirely different?

Like: "Do you think Robert and Carl will still pay us?"

"No."

Or: "When is it going to stop raining?"

"Stupid question."

Or: "Do you think Emily Hargraves will be MVP again this year?"

"Stop the questions already."

Somehow, by Sunday evening, River still hadn't told Zack.

On Monday morning parts of the coastal highway were closed due to flooding. All the fishermen up and down the coast stayed home. An entire pier near Azalea had been ripped from its mooring. For once River hoped that school wasn't canceled, and luckily, it wasn't.

All morning she thought about the A-Team practice that afternoon. She couldn't wait to tell the Hoop Girlz. At lunch, brimming with her news, she carried her tray to the table where Erica, Jennifer, and Wilfred sat.

But the minute she sat down, something stopped her from saying anything.

They all had glum faces. Maybe they'd all wanted to play in the tournament as much as she had. Maybe they wouldn't be so happy for her, after all.

"This afternoon," Jennifer said, "the Hoop Girlz should have a team-spirit meeting. Zack said teamwork is our greatest strength."

"Will Zack still coach us at the tournament, even if we don't get to practice anymore?" Wilfred asked.

"It's pouring," River said. "It's gonna pour all week. We aren't going to be able to practice, not even one day."

"Maybe the forecast is wrong," Erica said.

"Zack showed us good plays," Jennifer said. "We got to practice them for three days. We're all set for the tournament, anyway. Rain or shine."

"I don't know," River said. "We probably should cancel our spot in the tournament. I mean, we haven't even tried out the plays against a defense."

"Cancel our spot in the tournament? Are you crazy?" Erica shouted. She looked at Wilfred and Jennifer. "What's wrong with River?" Then she started singing, "Hoop Girlz just want to have fun, fun, fun." Wilfred and Jennifer joined in and they were so loud that everyone in the cafeteria looked at them.

"I don't know," River said again. "Without getting to practice, maybe we shouldn't play in the tournament."

"We're playing," Jennifer said. "Meet after school in the cafeteria for our team-spirit meeting." Then to Wilfred, "Want my spinach?"

At the end of the day, River spent a long

time packing her books in her knapsack. She didn't want the Hoop Girlz to see her going to the gym. She took the long way so she didn't have to pass the cafeteria. Finally, she ducked into the locker room.

A brown bag with her name on it sat on one of the locker-room benches. Inside was a brand new, red and white T-shirt with *Borowitz-Jacobs* printed on the back.

"Wow," she whispered, holding up the T-shirt. "Just like in the WNBA."

"Hey!" Kammie blurted. "River has an A-Team jersey! Where'd you get that?"

"Coach Glover asked me to be on the team," she said.

"Cool!" Kammie beamed. "This team is so boring. Maybe it'll be more fun now."

"Hi, River," Sarah said. "We do need more players."

"What happened to the Whoopie Girls?" Jeannie asked.

"Hoop Girlz," River said.

"Well, I hope you like passing the ball," Marianne put in, "because that's all you get to do on this team."

Rochelle kept her head down, her face

behind the veil of white blond hair, then shut her locker quietly and headed out to the gym.

"Pass to Rochelle, pass to Rochelle," Marianne said.

River wondered if the Hoop Girlz had begun their team-spirit meeting. They were probably singing their song.

She stepped out of the locker room and onto the basketball court. This is it, she thought. The beginning of my career. We're going to win the Oregon Coast Tournament. Emily Hargraves is going to scout me. I'm on my way to the WNBA.

River started shooting baskets to warm up. But something was wrong. Her feet felt like weights and she couldn't hit a thing. She glanced at Coach Glover who stood on the sidelines, his arms crossed on his chest.

River concentrated on her shot. But her hands felt cold and rubbery, as if they didn't even belong to her.

Where was the kingdom of basketball? She glanced around, as if she could find a gateway leading there. The gym was so warm and dry. There were plexiglass backboards, polished to a luster, rather than rusty metal ones. The nets were clean and bright white, no holes. She ought to be able to find her way into the kingdom from here.

River looked around again and her gaze landed on the door to the outside court. She went over and pushed it open. The rain fell, splatting into the lake on the court. The storm had torn one of the nets loose from the hoop. It hung limply. Still, that was the Hoop Girlz's court. The sight of it gave her a shot of energy. She turned back toward the gym, ready to give 100 percent.

But a funny thing happened. She set the basketball on the floor. She marched back into the locker room. She stripped off the red and white jersey. She quickly redressed in her street clothes and grabbed her own basketball. Then she went out to find Coach Glover in the gym.

She handed him the jersey. "I've decided to stick with the Hoop Girlz."

Coach Glover looked very surprised. He said, "Don't cut off your nose to spite your face, River. This is a big opportunity for you."

The shirt hung from his hand. She could see the first letters of her name on it.

"Thanks," she said. "I appreciate your giving me the chance. But I have other plans."

"You're making a big mistake," Coach Glover warned. "Quitting will get you nowhere, River."

River looked Coach Glover in the eye. "I'm not quitting," she said. "I'm sticking with the team I started." That feeling she had, of being ready to give 100 percent, wasn't for this team. It was for the Hoop Girlz.

She didn't wait to hear what Coach Glover had to say next. She ran to the door to the outside court, pushed it open, and threw herself out in the rain. River dribbled her ball to the hoop, splashing through the two-inch deep lake. In an instant her hair, jacket, and sneakers were drenched. She shot from the corner and sunk the shot.

River threw back her head and yelled, "Stop raining! Just stop!"

It didn't stop raining, but the outside court lights blinked on.

After shooting for a few minutes, River

checked the cafeteria, but the Hoop Girlz had already left. So she walked home slowly. The storm had torn one side of the Emily Hargraves banner from the lamppost to which it had been attached. That part of the banner laid in a wet pile on the sidewalk. River bent down beside it. As her hands touched the slippery plastic, some words—her own words—sprung into her mind. *It's practically as big as a basketball court.*

The haunted mansion ballroom.

"Thank you Basketball Court Goddess!" River cried up to the roiling clouds.

Then she ran the whole way home in lieu of that day's workout. Without even changing out of her wet clothes, she called Jennifer.

"I'm sorry I missed the team-spirit meeting," River said.

"We heard. You're on the A-Team now," Jennifer answered coldly. "It's okay. I understand. We all wanted to be on the A-Team."

"No, I'm not on the A-Team. I'm on the Hoop Girlz. I have an idea. But I have to talk to your dad."

"My dad?"

"Yeah, is he home?"

"Sure. He works the night shift. He's always home during the day."

"I know. Can I talk to him?"

A minute later the sheriff answered. "River. What can I do for you?"

River told him about all the phone calls she had made looking for a basketball court to use. Then she told the sheriff her idea.

"I was wondering if we would get arrested if, like in the daytime, not at night, we used the haunted mansion ballroom for Hoop Girlz practice."

"But there are no baskets there," the sheriff pointed out.

"It'd be better than nothing. It's big and dry. We could do drills and run our plays. So that our muscles will keep them memorized."

"Let me make a couple of phone calls," he said.

11. PURPLE SATIN

Riding to school the next day, Kammie was quiet for a long time. Finally, she asked, "Why did you quit the A-Team?"

"The A-Team?" Zack asked.

"I'm playing for the Hoop Girlz," River said.

"You'd rather play for the Hoop Girlz?" Kammie asked.

"Yep."

"Is there something you didn't tell me?" Zack asked.

"Get out, kids," Carolyn said, pulling up to the school sidewalk. "You're late."

When River got to the cafeteria at lunch, Jennifer was waiting for her. She rolled over at top speed, forcing a couple of kids to jump aside. "River!" she said. "My dad set it all up! He's going to take us over there after school."

"Cool!" River said.

"Over where?" Kammie appeared at River's side.

"It's a Hoop Girlz secret."

Kammie plunked her tray down at the Hoop Girlz's lunch table. Jennifer whispered the plan to Erica and Wilfred.

When the last bell rang, River grabbed her knapsack and hurried toward the back door of the school.

Once again, Kammie was at her side. "Can I ask you a question?"

"I'm sort of busy now."

Erica ran up and grabbed River's arm. "Come on. The sheriff says to hurry."

"What did you do?" Kammie asked, running alongside River and Erica.

"Nothing," River said. "Don't you have practice now?"

"That's what I want to talk about. I want to play for the Hoop Girlz."

"What do you mean?" River turned to face her. "You're on the A-Team."

"You guys have much more fun. All the A-Team does is set up Rochelle to look good. Everyone is so mad."

As the girls stepped outside, they saw the sheriff's truck.

"River!" Jennifer called as her dad and Zack lifted her and her wheelchair into the truck. "Let's go!"

River ran to the sheriff's truck where the rest of the team was already waiting. Erica climbed in behind her.

"Ready to go?" asked the sheriff, gunning the engine a bit.

"What's Kammie doing here?" Zack asked, looking out the truck window.

Kammie stood in the parking lot, rain streaming off the ends of her hair. She knocked on the truck window and Zack rolled it down a couple of inches.

"I want to play for the Hoop Girlz," she said again. "Can I?"

"She's a really good player," Jennifer said. "We need more players."

Wilfred scowled, looking afraid of Kammie.

"Zack is the coach," Erica said. "He should decide."

Zack said, "We don't tolerate ball hogs on the Hoop Girlz. If you think you're going to be some kind of star, forget it."

"I know," Kammie said, speaking softly for once. "I won't hog the ball. I just want to play with you guys."

River shrugged at her brother.

"She is really good," Jennifer repeated.

"As long as you're coachable," Zack warned. "I don't work with uncoachable athletes."

"Yeah," Wilfred put in. "He's a lot tougher than Coach Glover, so don't think you're going to get off easy."

"I can handle that," Kammie declared. "I've had professional experience."

"Oh, boy," River said. But Jennifer was right: Kammie was good. Now they would have five players, a full team. They would only have to use Megan as a substitute.

"Get in," Zack said, rolling up his window and opening the truck door.

The sheriff turned on the red swirling

rooftop light. He smiled his jowly smile in the rearview mirror. "My shift doesn't start for a few more hours," he explained, "but the Hoop Girlz deserve the full treatment."

Heading out of the school parking lot, River felt as if the Hoop Girlz were the guests of honor in a parade. When they reached the back road leading to the haunted mansion, the sheriff turned on the siren.

"It's an emergency!" he cried. "The Hoop Girlz have only three days to practice for the tournament!"

River wondered if sheriffs could be arrested. He kept the truck wailing and flashing all the way to the haunted mansion.

"Oh, no!" River groaned when they got there. A fire truck was parked on the high-way in front of the big house. Two firefight-ers were hauling a long structure across the field.

Had she and Zack left the lantern in the ballroom? Had it started a fire?

That was impossible. It was pouring rain. There wasn't a lick of flame or a puff of smoke in sight. There couldn't be a fire.

"Good," said the sheriff, driving up the overgrown driveway, right to the front door, and pulling on the parking brake. "They're on time."

He jumped out of the truck and greeted the two firefighters. River saw now that what they carried was a portable basketball hoop. The sheriff opened the door to the haunted mansion. With a great deal of difficulty, the firefighters wrestled the basket and stand through the door.

The kids all clamored in after them, with Zack and the sheriff lifting Jennifer and her wheelchair over the threshold.

"Thanks, men," the sheriff said.

One of the firefighters cleared her throat.

"And, uh, ladies," the sheriff corrected with a chuckle.

She rolled her eyes.

The sheriff clapped his hands and rubbed them vigorously. "We'll return it soon. I'm sure you all can amuse yourselves at the station with cards or dominoes for a few days."

"Just remember," the woman said. "You owe us one, Sheriff. Getting this hoop over here was a pain in the neck. It's too big to fit in anyone's pickup, so we had to use the retired fire truck. Let's go, Mac."

"Wait," Zack said. "Don't leave yet. We really need to practice against a defense."

The two firefighters looked at each other.

"Excellent idea," the sheriff agreed. "Stay."

"We go on duty in an hour," Mac said. "Sorry."

"An hour is plenty of time," the sheriff told him.

"Look," Mac said. "This is a favor, okay? We're loaning you the station basketball hoop for a couple of days. That's it. Let's go, Zelda."

The woman laced her fingers together and stretched out her arms. "I had quite a jump shot in college," she allowed.

"Zelda," her partner said. "We can't—"

"You two," Zack said, counting, "the sheriff. Me. And Megan. That's a defensive team. Just one hour."

"Please," all the Hoop Girlz begged.

"I'm a firefighter," Mac said, "not a little girls' basketball coach."

"No one's asking you to be the coach," Zack said. "*I'm* the coach."

"Ah, come on, Mac," Zelda said. "Just give them an hour. What else are you going to do in the hour we have before work? It'll be good for you, a little exercise." She whacked him in the paunch.

Zack and the sheriff pushed the portable basket to the end of the ballroom. River used the broom the sheriff had brought to clear the floor of dust bunnies and grit. In daylight, with the sheriff, firefighters, and Hoop Girlz all here, the haunted mansion wasn't even a little bit scary. It was just a big old run-down house.

Zack showed the plays to Kammie, and within minutes they were scrimmaging.

Sweating through his light tan uniform, the sheriff threw himself into playing defense. Mac, the firefighter, walked through the motions, but he wasn't happy about it. Zelda, the firefighter, on the other hand, seemed to forget she was playing with kids. She played so heartily that Zack had to ask her to let the Hoop Girlz get some rebounds so they could practice their plays.

"They can jump for them, can't they?" Zelda asked.

"They're, like, a few feet shorter than you," Mac reminded her.

"Oh," she said as if waking up from a dream. "Oh, okay." Then, "Hey, Mac, we should start a station team. Play in a league or something. This is fun."

Mac sighed and got into position again.

Every afternoon for the rest of that week, the sheriff drove the Hoop Girlz to the timber baron's house. Every day Zelda showed up to play for an hour before her shift, though Mac refused to come again. The Hoop Girlz worked on their plays, running them dozens of times.

"It's called muscle memory," Jennifer told her dad when he complained about doing the same thing over and over.

"Take it from the top," Zack ordered.

On Friday, the day before the start of the tournament, Zack told the girls—as well as the sheriff and Zelda—that they would only scrimmage for a few minutes. He wanted the team to be fully rested for the tournament the next day.

At the end of Friday's practice, Wilfred dropped a big bag in the middle of the ballroom floor. "I have a surprise. My mom made these. River, yours is on top."

River reached into the bag and felt a slick, soft fabric. She pulled out a deep purple satin basketball jersey. On the front and back was the number 10. Across the back shoulders, in white satin letters, it said, *Hoop Girlz.* Below her number, the satin lettering spelled out *Borowitz-Jacobs.*

Wilfred reached into the bag and pulled out a pair of purple satin shorts to match. "My mom made complete uniforms for everyone on the team."

River held the uniform against her face. "She sewed all of these? Even the numbers and names?"

"Yeah, but, um, we could wear the silk-screened ones instead," Wilfred stammered. "I mean, these don't replace those or any-thing. They're just extra."

River said, "Are you kidding? Every team needs practice jerseys and game uniforms. There's no way we could have shown up at the tournament in those T-shirts we've been wearing for a month."

"Yeah," Erica agreed, petting the purple satin fabric of her own jersey.

"There's one for me, too!" Megan squealed.

Kammie twisted a strand of hair. "I don't need a uniform."

"Sorry," Wilfred said. "We didn't know you were on the team."

"They're kind of dumb looking, anyway," Kammie said.

"All right," Zack interrupted, sounding especially gruff. "We need to talk about basketball, not clothes. I want you at the gym tomorrow at 8:00 sharp."

"Just a sec," Wilfred said, reaching to the bottom of the bag. "This is for you."

She held up a deep purple satin jacket. Across the back shoulders, in white satin lettering, it said, *Coach Borowitz-Jacobs*.

Zack rubbed his chin to hide his smile.

"Hoop Girlz rule!" Jennifer called out, raising a fist. All the other girls—and even the sheriff, Zelda, and Zack—raised their fists and answered, "Hoop Girlz rule!"

12. THE TOURNAMENT

On Saturday morning, River, Zack, and Kammie were the first to arrive for the tournament. River took a deep breath as she stepped into the gym. She could feel her purple satin uniform swishing under her warm-ups as she walked across the shiny floor.

Coach Glover had posted the tournament schedule on the gym wall.

Hoop Girlz	Lincoln	A-Team
vs.	vs.	vs.
Agate Beach	Clark Cougars	Seaside
Saturday, 9:00 A.M.	Saturday, 12:00 noon	Saturday, 3:00 P.M.

bye   Semifinals
Sunday, 11:00 A.M.

Finals
Sunday, 2:00 P.M.

"Hey, Coach Glover got the name of our team right."

"Yeah, and check it out," Zack said. "You have a bye in the second round. Meaning, after you beat Agate Beach, you go straight to the finals."

"Where's Emily Hargraves?" Kammie asked, looking around as if the star of the WNBA was hiding under the bleachers.

"She probably won't come until the finals," Zack said.

"That's stupid," Kammie said. "If she came today, she could see all the teams and choose the MVP. In fact, she wouldn't have to look farther than the first game."

"What if we don't make it to the finals?" River asked her brother. "Then Emily Hargraves won't even see the Hoop Girlz play."

"You'll make it to the finals," Zack growled in his deep coach voice. "You have to. My honor is on the line."

"Yeah," Kammie agreed. "Mine, too. River, there is no if about this game. We're winning. You'd better get that in your head."

Just then the rest of the Hoop Girlz came into the gym. Wilfred handed a neatly folded purple satin bundle to Kammie, saying, "My mom made your uniform last night."

Kammie shouted, "Hah!" and, grinning, ran to the locker room to change.

"I thought she said they were 'dumb looking,'" Erica commented.

Zack called a team meeting. He explained that he expected the Hoop Girlz to make it to the finals, and that he was sure they would be playing the A-Team in that game. Therefore, he didn't want them to run any of their plays in this first round. He didn't want to give away their secrets. The Hoop Girlz were to simply play the best basketball they could against Agate Beach.

"But without my play, I probably won't be able to get my shot off," Jennifer protested.

"I know," Zack said. "But we need to save your shot for the big game. So we can surprise the A-Team. Now get out there and play your best basketball. That's all I'm asking this morning."

"In other words," Kammie said, "let's kick butt."

There weren't too many spectators for this first game of the tournament, but the Hoop

Girlz had some supporters. River's parents were there. Wilfred's parents came as well. Erica's mom showed up wearing warm-ups, high-top sneakers, and even a sweatband, like she was planning on coming in as a sub. Jennifer and Megan's mom was there with the sheriff in his street clothes. Robert and Carl came to heckle Zack. Even Zelda, the firefighter, showed up.

When the Hoop Girlz stripped off their sweats to warm up, a soft chorus of *oooohs* and *aaaahs* drifted down onto the court. River knew the spectators were admiring the purple satin uniforms. She noticed that Jennifer had brand new purple sneakers to match, too. Which was pretty funny because her completely limp feet didn't work at all. Still, Jennifer wore her new purple high-tops as if they would launch her right out of her wheelchair for rebounds.

As the Hoop Girlz began running their warm-up drills, the coach of the Agate Beach team approached Zack. She looked nervous. "Uh, are there any adults working with this team?"

"I'm the coach," Zack said. "What can I do for you?"

"Uh, the girl in the wheelchair . . . I'm afraid we can't consent to her playing in the tournament." The woman tried to speak softly, but her voice carried across the court. Everyone heard her.

Zack was silent, not knowing what to say.

"Who are you?" Kammie shouted over to the woman. "She's one of the Hoop Girlz and you'll just have to get used to it, lady."

"Be quiet, Kammie," Zack said, but he looked like he had wanted to say the same thing to the Agate Beach coach.

Coach Glover strode onto the court and asked, "What's the problem here? Everyone ready to start the game?"

The Agate Beach coach explained, "I think there's a liability problem here. If the young lady in the wheelchair gets hurt, someone may be responsible. I don't think we can allow her to play."

River watched Coach Glover carefully. He straightened his back. "As organizer of this tournament," he stated, "I rule that Jennifer has every right to play. And the Agate Beach team has every right to withdraw from the tournament, if it wishes."

The Agate Beach coach looked angry, but she mumbled, "We'll play."

"Begin the game," Coach Glover ordered the refs.

Erica went to center court for the tip-off. River stood ready to get the tip. Jennifer waited under the basket. They hoped to get the first bucket of the game. The ref held up the ball. The gym was perfectly silent.

Except for the sound of the side door opening and shutting with a loud clang. A young woman with honey-colored hair and legs so long she could climb the bleachers three at a time, slipped inside and quickly found a seat.

"Emily Hargraves," River whispered. It was Emily Hargraves in person. She had come for the first round of the tournament.

River closed her eyes and thought, even if we lose every game in the tournament, I will have been scouted by the MVP of the WNBA.

"River!" Kammie screamed.

River opened her eyes just as the basketball sailed past her head. Erica had tipped the ball perfectly, right to her. But she had had her eyes shut and missed the tip.

Agate Beach gained first possession of the ball.

Zack yelled from the sidelines, "Wake up, River!"

She heard Robert and Carl howling with laughter.

Zelda, the firefighter, called out, "Look alive, Hoop Girlz!"

In fact, just about everyone in the stands yelled something.

Luckily, the Agate Beach point guard missed her shot. Erica got the rebound, and Kammie took the ball down court for the Hoop Girlz. When she reached the three-point line she stopped. River couldn't believe she was going to try to shoot from there. Besides, Jennifer was wide open.

Sure enough, Kammie gunned a shot from the three-point line. It didn't even make it to the hoop. River jumped in front of her opponent. She snagged the missed shot. Then she bounce passed to Jennifer.

Jennifer held the ball in her lap for a moment, waiting for someone to guard her. No Agate Beach player stepped forward. Jennifer pushed the ball toward the basket with her two-handed shot, and it fell in.

River saw the point guard for Agate Beach look over at her coach on the bench. The coach shook her head.

Agate Beach started down the court with the ball. As the girl with the ball crossed the center line, Kammie sprinted toward her. Like a hawk, Kammie swooped past, snatching the ball. She turned and drove all the way to the Hoop Girlz bucket and laid in another easy two.

Kammie whooped and raised her fist in the air. All the Hoop Girlz sang their song. The audience laughed.

That made Agate Beach mad. They got serious and made two straight baskets.

Jennifer hissed, "Pass the ball," to Kammie as the Hoop Girlz headed down court to their own basket again.

They set up their offense. Jennifer rocketed toward the key. The defense scattered. She sat in her wheelchair completely alone in the key, absolutely wide open.

"I'm open!" she yelled to Kammie.

Rather than passing, though, Kammie used the opportunity of the open key for herself. She drove in for an easy layup.

"Hah!" she cried, raising her fist again.

At the beginning of the second half, the score was tied. In the first play River snagged a rebound. She was open, so she went up for the shot. The ball hit the rim, rolled around it two whole times, and then slid off the outside. Agate Beach got the rebound, took off for a fast break, and made two more points. A minute later they scored again.

Trotting back down the court, River glanced up in the stands at Emily Hargraves again. It was no use. They were going to lose in the first round.

"River!" About five people screamed her name. She looked up in time to see the ball fly past her head and out of bounds. Again.

After that, Kammie took the game completely into her own hands. She stole the ball two more times and made six more points.

"I'm open!" Jennifer kept calling out.

"I'm the one who stole the ball," Kammie answered. "So I get to take the shot."

The Hoop Girlz won, by three points.

"Hoop Girlz just want to have fun, fun, fun," Erica sang, but no one else wanted to celebrate.

"She promised she wouldn't be a ball hog," Jennifer said angrily.

"Look," Zack said, "the truth is, Kammie won that game for us. Barely. Her steals and baskets were crucial."

"Yeah!" Kammie agreed.

Jennifer rolled her eyes.

River complained, "If she had passed, then maybe some of the rest of us could have scored, too."

"I was wide open the whole time," Jennifer said. "They were afraid to guard me. Kammie should have passed to me. We didn't even need to use the play. I could have scored as much as she did."

"I'm glad she didn't pass to me," Wilfred said, hugging herself tightly.

"Watch out, WNBA!" Kammie crowed. "Here comes Kammie Wilder!"

Zack nodded slowly. "We won, okay? Tomorrow, you're going to have to play as a team, or you'll lose. That means you'll have to show leadership, Kammie. As point guard, it's going to be your job to *set up* the plays."

"That means no ball hogging," Erica translated.

"That means passing the ball," Jennifer clarified.

"To Jennifer," Wilfred corrected. "Not to me."

"Wilfred," Zack said sternly. "We'll need your speed. And your speed is no good unless you make your shots. So Kammie will pass the ball to you, too."

Wilfred bit her lip.

"All right," Zack said. "I want you all to go home and have naps."

"Naps?" Kammie said. "No way."

"I mean it," he said. "And no candy or potato chips or sodas tonight, either. Healthy food only, got it?"

"Easy for you to say, Mr. Lentil Loaf," Kammie said.

Zack took both of Kammie's shoulders in his hands. "Don't think I'll be afraid to bench you tomorrow. Megan can go in for you. Agate

Beach wasn't all that good. The A-Team is. There is only one way to beat them: team-work. Think about it."

Before leaving the gym, River looked up at the fans crowding Emily Hargraves. She wanted to go up to her, but there were too many people. What would she say, anyway?

Of course Kammie bounded right up the bleachers. River watched her elbow through the knot of people and hand Emily a pen and her basketball. She watched Emily smile at Kammie and ask her some questions. Then Kammie sat down, right on the bench next to Emily, as if she were her sister or something.

After changing, River met her parents and Zack at the car.

"Where's Kammie?" her mother asked.

"With Emily Hargraves," River said sulkily.

"Why don't you run in and get her?"

"Oh, right," River said. "You try. Getting Kammie away from Emily Hargraves would be like trying to drag a dog away from a steak."

"She can walk home," Zack said.

"Exactly," River agreed.

The next day, all the Hoop Girlz sat with Zack in the bleachers. Zack spoke to them quietly throughout the semifinal game. Together they studied the A-Team.

Rochelle got practically every rebound. A lot of her shots fell in, too. Even if the Hoop Girlz double-teamed her, she could shoot over their heads. Besides, the rest of the team looked so disciplined. They played a tight zone defense. Their passes were quick and accurate.

"But they have to play two games today," Kammie pointed out. "We'll be rested."

"It might help," Zack said cautiously.

River doubted it. The A-Team had done all that intense conditioning. Coach Glover sat on the bench, looking completely confident. She bet he figured the A-Team could beat the Hoop Girlz, even if they had played five games that day. River wished Zack hadn't asked them to come early. Watching the A-Team only scared her. They won the semifinals easily.

By two o'clock, the bleachers were packed for the final game. Everyone in town came to the game. They'd all heard about Wally

Glover, the ex-NBA player, and his daughter, Rochelle, who just might be the next Emily Hargraves. Most of all, though, everyone knew Emily herself would be at the game.

That afternoon she had her own special box seat, front and center. The town mayor and his wife sat with the star of the WNBA. The box was marked off with a set of red and white helium balloons flying from each corner.

Coach Glover had posted a huge sheet of butcher paper on one wall. Down the left side, he listed the names of all the players in the final game, the A-Team first, followed by the Hoop Girlz. Across the top, he made columns for *points, rebounds,* and *assists.* Everyone would be able to see the final game statistics.

When the Hoop Girlz began warming up, the air in the gym was already hot, moist, and electric. River figured her parents had finally started to understand the importance of basketball, because her mom had sliced up a dozen organic oranges and put them on plates behind the Hoop Girlz bench. Her dad wore three cameras around his neck and was already roaming the gym, checking the lighting and looking for good angles.

As the A-Team shot baskets on their own side of the court, River heard Jeannie say, "I can't believe the Whoopie Girls made it to the finals."

"It's because Coach Glover felt sorry for them," Marianne answered. "He gave them that bye in the second round. All they had to do was beat Agate Beach, and anyone could have done that."

Sarah chanted, "Drive to the left, drive to the *right,* the A-Team girls have the meanest *bite.*"

"Hah!" Kammie snorted. She yelled across the gym, "Drive to the left, drive to the *right,* the A-Team girls have nothing but *height.*"

The A-Team was quiet for a moment, then Marianne whooped, "One, two, three, *four,* Azalea A-Team is gonna score, score, *score.*"

This time Erica answered, "One, two, three, *four,* Azalea A-Team is one big *bore.*"

Jeannie walked to center court, stopping

at the line there, as if it were a fence. She shouted, "All the other teams had better *run*, because Azalea A-Team is number *one*!"

Kammie headed for Jeannie. But Zack grabbed her by the purple satin of her jersey and pulled her back to the Hoop Girlz bench. "If I catch any of you thinking about anything but basketball from here on out," he threatened, "I'm quitting."

Kammie shut up, but River couldn't keep herself from shouting across the court, "It's the A-Team who had better *run*, because the Hoop Girlz have a lot more *fun*."

"River!" Zack said.

"Well, they're so arrogant."

Zack shook his head and called the Hoop Girlz into a huddle.

He told Kammie, "You're my point guard. That means you're in charge of the plays."

"I know."

"That means you have to know when to pass."

"I know."

"That means listen for directions."

"I know."

"See that chart of stats up there?"

Kammie nodded.

"The best point guard in this game will have the most assists."

Jennifer said, "An assist is when you see someone open, you pass to them, and they make the shot."

"Duh," Kammie said.

"Got that?" Zack asked her.

She nodded solemnly.

River and Jennifer exchanged looks. Winning would be nearly impossible. To simply do well, everyone had to play her best. River had to be aggressive. Erica had to get serious. Wilfred had to not be afraid. Jennifer had to be able to get her shot off. Most of all, Kammie had to show leadership.

Unfortunately, this game didn't start out any better than the one against Agate Beach. Rochelle, being six inches taller than Erica, got the tip-off. The A-Team took the ball to the hoop and scored.

In fact, they scored six points in the first five minutes.

No matter how hard they tried, the Hoop

Girlz weren't able to score. The A-Team had a wicked defense. Unlike Agate Beach, they weren't afraid to guard Jennifer tightly. It was impossible to get the ball to her. Erica looked like she was in a dream most of the time, and Wilfred was visibly shaking. For a while Kammie did pass the ball. But every time River got it, an A-Team player would be right in her face. Once she got so nervous, she just handed the ball to her opponent.

Only Kammie was unruffled. She kept giving the signals for their plays. But none of the other Hoop Girlz got into position. Finally, Kammie got frustrated and once again began gunning shots every time she got the ball. But there was no use in that, either. The A-Team knew she had a good shot. They double-teamed her as soon as she started shooting.

At halftime, the score was A-Team, 14, and Hoop Girlz, 4.

As River walked off the court with her team, she felt sick. They were playing terribly. Robert and Carl were shouting insults to her brother about his coaching. The fans were stomping and cheering for the A-Team.

River wanted to take a shower and go home.

13. ORANGE RIM, WHITE NET

After halftime, the A-Team ran single file onto the court as if they were troops rather than basketball players. They ran a lap around the gym, then circled into a huddle, where they high-fived, as if they'd already won the tournament title.

The Hoop Girlz gathered into their own huddle. The only thing Zack said was, "Do me a favor. *Run the plays.*"

The A-Team got the tip-off and drove for the basket. They missed.

River brought down the rebound. She heard her brother's voice screaming, "The fast-break play!"

Wilfred flew down the court. River cranked back her arm and heaved the ball. It sailed over center court, right for Wilfred. She was all alone under the basket, but she still looked terrified. Her arms and legs seemed to freeze. Even her face froze in one expression. The ball slammed, right on target, into her stomach. And knocked her out.

Mrs. Sanders screamed from the bleachers.

A couple of the A-Team girls laughed, thinking she had just fallen over.

Wilfred didn't get up. She was out cold.

The ref called a time-out, and someone's mom who was a doctor rushed down to the court. Wilfred soon sat up. She only had had the wind knocked out of her.

"Oh, boy," Jennifer mumbled to River. "That's the end of the fast-break play. Wilfred will pass out if someone *dribbles* the ball near her."

"Megan," Zack growled. "Go in for Wilfred."

"Look," Jeannie shrieked. "It's some-body's baby sister!"

"What about *my* play?" Jennifer urged. "Shouldn't we run that?"

"Not yet," Zack said firmly. "Wait until Wilfred is back in."

"I know the play," Megan said indignantly.

She marched over and whispered something to Jennifer. Jennifer rolled over and whispered to Kammie. Kammie nodded.

A minute later River pulled down another rebound. Without Wilfred to sprint to their basket, she passed to Kammie to take the ball down court. Kammie raised her fist, the signal for Jennifer's play.

Little Megan ran to her sister's defender and planted herself. Jennifer whipped around the surprised defensive player, and Kammie fired her the ball. Jennifer shot and hit gold. Two points!

Zack didn't even get angry at Megan and Jennifer for going against his orders. He jumped in the air, swinging his fist. "Yes!" he cried.

"Big deal. Two measly points," Marianne said.

But when a young woman's voice shouted, "Nice *play*, Hoop Girlz!" every single girl on that court looked up in the bleachers to see if it was she. It was. Emily Hargraves was on her feet, applauding the Hoop Girlz's play.

"So they made a basket," Jeannie mumbled.

But Emily Hargraves's praise unhinged something in the A-Team. River practically saw the nuts and bolts come loose in their game. Each of the girls wanted that praise for herself. After all, they must have reasoned, they were winning by a landslide. It couldn't hurt if someone other than the coach's daughter got some of the credit.

They stopped passing to Rochelle. No matter how much Coach Glover yelled from the sidelines, they didn't pass to her. The A-Team girls all started hogging the ball. They started gunning wild shots from anywhere on the court. They only passed when there was no other choice.

Of course, with her height, Rochelle still got a lot of the rebounds. And even with Erica and River double-teaming her, she still made points.

But the Hoop Girlz began to score more. Like the time Kammie took the ball down court and had an open shot. But she saw that Erica was free right under the basket. She passed. Erica's shot tapped the backboard and fell in.

"An assist!" Kammie hollered to the person marking the stats on the chart. "Mark down an assist for Kammie Wilder!"

After that, Kammie had a hunger for assists. She knew she wouldn't be able to catch Rochelle in rebounds or points. But she realized that she could be good at passing to open people. Since she had a reputation for always shooting, no one expected her to pass. Which made the assists all that more successful.

Meanwhile, the A-Team players were getting angry with one another for ball hogging. They argued on the court. They ignored Coach Glover yelling from the sidelines. The gap in the score closed a little bit. With ten minutes to go, it was A-Team, 21, and Hoop Girlz, 14.

Kammie intercepted a wild pass. "Someone should be keeping stats on steals!" she yelled over her shoulder as she took the ball down court. She passed to River.

River looked over the situation. The key was crowded. The defense was in place. She hesitated, then she hesitated some more. Before she knew it, an A-Team player reached out and simply plucked the ball out of her hands.

The A-Team ran a fast-break play and scored.

Kammie grabbed River's arm. "What's wrong with you? Look at the score! We're losing. Quit playing like a wimp. You have to get *mad.*"

"Don't be so competitive. Leave me alone." River wrenched her arm free.

"River," Kammie said as if she were astonished at how dense River was being. "Do you know who's sitting up there?" Kammie pointed right at Emily Hargraves in the bleachers.

River tried to ignore Kammie. But she couldn't help looking to where she pointed. There was Emily Hargraves, MVP of the WNBA, leaning forward with her elbows on her knees. Her gray eyes looked right at River. Maybe she even nodded.

"Get mad," Kammie repeated as she took the ball down court. She fired the ball to River.

River looked for an open player. No one was in position to shoot.

She took a deep breath of the moist gym

air. She spread her fingers around the ball, feeling each little nub on the leather. She looked up at the basket, and the door opened. River *knew* there were two defensive players between her and the hoop, but she didn't *see* them. She saw only that orange rim and the white net.

Afterward, she couldn't remember how she got past the defense. All she remembered was popping the ball against the backboard and seeing it drop in. Then the roar that went up in the stands. The sound of cymbals crashing. A ref blew his whistle. Not only had she worked her way around two defenders to make the shot, she had been fouled.

Standing on the free-throw line, River bounced the ball a couple of times to steady herself. What had driven her straight through the A-Team defense? Killer instinct?

No, it was the kingdom of basketball.

River bent her knees and shot. The ball arced high and fell in. All net.

Her three points brought the score to A-Team, 23, and Hoop Girlz, 17. With five minutes to go in the game.

"It was a fluke," Jeannie said. "She couldn't do that again."

Then she did.

The Hoop Girlz gained possession and set up their defense. Kammie passed to Erica who faked a pass to Wilfred. While the A-Team laughed at Wilfred flinching, Erica fired the ball to River. The minute she wrapped her fingers around the ball, the gateway opened up in front of her, the gateway to the kingdom of basketball. River popped in a short jumper. Catching on too late, an A-Team player tried to block the shot and fouled her.

River was on the free-throw line again. She sunk the shot, for another three-point play.

A-Team, 23, and Hoop Girlz, 20. Three minutes to go in the game.

The crowd was on its feet, roaring. Roaring for River who had just made six points in two minutes.

Coach Glover called another time-out.

"Keep it up," Zack told the Hoop Girlz. "Keep running the plays."

As they walked back out onto the court,

Kammie said, "See? I told you. You have to get mad."

"I didn't get mad. I went through a secret door."

"Huh?" Kammie said.

Coach Glover must have scared the A-Team. They passed the ball to their post, Rochelle. She made a shot. With only a minute to go, the score was 25 to 20.

The next time someone tried to pass to Rochelle, Kammie dove for the ball. Her body flew practically horizontal to the ground. She grabbed the ball right out of the air. "Go, Wilfred!" she hollered.

Wilfred sprinted for the Hoop Girlz basket. Kammie fired the ball like a bullet. River held her breath. Suddenly Wilfred's hands flew up like she was going to karate chop someone. The ball flew into her chest. She wrapped her arms around it. Wilfred caught the ball.

She turned toward the basket. The five A-Team players were running toward her. River saw Wilfred glance over her shoulder at them. Suddenly Wilfred shouted, "Hoop

Girlz rule!" and put the ball up and in the basket.

Another roar went up in the bleachers. The town band started playing as if the Hoop Girlz had just won the game. In fact, they were behind, 22 to 25.

The A-Team took the ball out of bounds. There were only thirty seconds to go in the game, so Coach Glover yelled, "Just keep possession! Just keep possession!"

But Kammie became the human vulture again. It seemed like she flew about fifty feet to intercept the inbounds pass. She went for the hoop, ready to shoot a layup. But Rochelle was right there with her long arms to block the shot.

Kammie passed off to Jennifer. Erica saw the opportunity and set a pick. Jennifer wheeled around the pick and made an easy shot. With ten seconds to go in the game, the score was Hoop Girlz, 24, and A-Team, 25.

This time the guard threw a loopty-loo pass over everyone's heads. Rochelle reached up and grabbed it. Then she held the ball over her head, waiting for the clock to run out.

"I'm not tall enough!" Kammie screamed, leaping up and down, trying to knock the ball out of Rochelle's hands. "Help!"

Jeannie pointed at the hopping Kammie and laughed. She laughed so hard, she had to bend over. Marianne and Sarah joined in. They were so busy laughing they didn't see Erica fly in from behind. Erica, the tallest of the Hoop Girlz, leaped and knocked the ball out of Rochelle's hands.

The ball rocketed right into Jennifer's lap.

Jennifer screamed, "Run, Wilfred!" and dished the ball to River.

River tossed the ball, and again, Wilfred caught the pass. But it was too late. The buzzer sounded and the game was over—just one second before Wilfred's shot fell in.

The A-Team had won, 25 to 24.

14. THE SECRET DOOR

The crowd was on its feet, stomping, clapping, shouting. Emily Hargraves, finally, was walking to center court. She took the microphone handed to her by Wally Glover. The two pro ball players shook hands. Then Coach Glover walked back to his bench.

River sat on her own team's bench, her elbows on her knees, her head in her hands. They had lost by one point. Just one point. It was almost worse than losing by a landslide.

The rest of her team didn't seem to think so. They were dancing to the music the band played, and singing the *Hoop Girlz just want to have fun, fun, fun* song. Even Kammie. Even competitive, killer instinct Kammie seemed delighted with herself. Sure, they'd played a great game in the second half, but they had lost.

As Emily Hargraves began to speak, River lifted her head to listen. Emily was trying to quiet the crowd, but the people wouldn't stop cheering and the band wouldn't stop playing.

River saw a pale blur, like a streaking ghost, run along the far wall of the gym and slip out the door.

"Did you see that?" River whispered to Kammie. "I think Rochelle just ran out of the gym."

"Probably went to the bathroom. She was probably afraid she'd pee on herself getting her trophy."

Coach Glover also walked along the edge of gym and stepped out.

Finally Emily Hargraves managed to quiet the spectators. "Thank you," she told her fans. "It's great to be back home and to see so many old friends. I can't tell you how much I enjoyed watching this tournament. I saw some amazingly polished skills for players so young. So with no further ado, I would like to present the Oregon Coast Tournament trophy to the Azalea A-Team. Come on out here, girls."

As the A-Team accepted its trophy, the girls glanced around, looking for Rochelle and Coach Glover.

Kammie leaned over and whispered to River, "I bet she wants to make a grand entrance for her MVP trophy. Watch, she'll probably come out wearing a crown or something."

Emily picked up the MVP trophy and smiled. She nodded at the big sheet of statistics that Coach Glover had posted. "You can't argue with statistics. I know that Rochelle Glover is going to make a big splash in the WNBA in a few years. Come on out here, Rochelle, MVP of the Oregon Coast Tournament."

Everyone looked around for Rochelle.

Kammie whispered to River, "On second thought, maybe she got so excited she's barfing in the bathroom."

Just in time, Coach Glover came through the door holding Rochelle's elbow. She wasn't wearing a crown. She hardly even raised her head. As she took her trophy, she looked like she wanted to cry.

Emily put an arm around Rochelle's shoulder and said, "I would also like the Hoop Girlz to join me at center court."

The Hoop Girlz all leaned forward on their bench and looked at one another. No one moved, until Kammie leaped up. "Come on, you guys." River, Erica, Wilfred, and Megan followed Kammie out to center court.

Jennifer grabbed Zack's hands and tried to pull him off the bench. He wouldn't budge, so she yelled to her teammates to help. The Hoop Girlz returned to the bench and lifted Zack right off it. They half carried, half dragged him to center court.

Emily waited for the cheering to die down. Then she looked at the team of six girls, if you counted Megan, and one boy, if you counted the coach. She shook her head and laughed. She told the crowd, "I'm going to be honest with you all. The Hoop Girlz don't have the breadth of skills that the A-Team has. They certainly don't have the height. But I saw another kind of talent on this team. A talent that is unusual among adults, and even more so among young players. Teamwork. The Hoop Girlz pulled off some great plays that overcame their disadvantages. They did this by working together and using each of their strengths. This was a very close game and the reason it was so close was because the Hoop Girlz played great team basketball."

"Do you think she'll mention my assists?" Kammie said right out loud to River.

River stepped gently on Kammie's foot to shut her up.

"I also had the most steals," she persisted.

"Be quiet," River whispered.

Emily continued, "For that reason, I award the title of MVP to both Rochelle Glover of the A-Team for her outstanding personal performance, and to the entire Hoop Girlz team for their outstanding teamwork. Congratulations, Rochelle Glover and the Hoop Girlz, Most Valuable Players of the tournament."

"What about trophies?" Kammie shouted to be heard above the cheering. "What about free basketball camp?"

Emily Hargraves placed a hand on Kammie's head. "I'll make sure some more trophies are made up so that each of you gets one. And Rochelle, as well as every one of the Hoop Girlz, will have a place at my basketball camp this summer."

"For free?"

"Absolutely."

"Woo hoo!" Kammie yelled out to the entire gym. She tossed her basketball high in the air, then twirled around underneath it until it fell back into her hands.

The tournament was over and fans swarmed onto the court.

The Hoop Girlz hugged one another and made plans to play hoops the next afternoon in the haunted mansion. River said they might as well take advantage of the firefighters' hoop, until Zelda or Mac came to get it. As they came out of their group hug, River noticed Rochelle standing a few feet away. She wasn't holding her MVP trophy.

"What do *you* want?" Kammie asked.

"I heard you say you were going to play hoops tomorrow."

"Just the Hoop Girlz," Kammie said. "We have a private court."

Rochelle looked at her feet. Then she looked up. "I know about your private court."

"You do?" River asked.

"The sheriff called my dad to ask if you could use it."

"Rochelle," Coach Glover said, approaching the girls. "You left your MVP trophy on the bench."

Rochelle ignored the trophy he held out to her.

"You don't want it, I'll take it," Kammie said.

Coach Glover cleared his throat. "Congratulations," he told River. "The Hoop Girls—"

"Zzz," River corrected.

Coach Glover looked confused.

Rochelle said, "Hoop Girlzzz, not Hoop Girlsss."

"Excuse me. As I was saying, The Hoop Girlzzz did a great job tonight. You really pulled through, River."

"Wait. Was it you who bought the haunted mansion?" she asked.

"It's haunted, is it?" Coach Glover laughed.

"Totally," Kammie said. "The place is crawling with ghosts and aliens."

River said, "And you told Jennifer's dad we could practice there."

"I guess that's right." He took Rochelle's elbow. "Come on, Rochelle. Emily said she'd spend a few minutes talking with us about your future."

"Figures," Kammie said.

"Not now," Rochelle said. "I'm talking with River and Kammie."

Coach Glover looked very surprised.

"Rochelle, this isn't the time for—"

"No," she repeated.

River studied the big man's face. "You turned on the outside court lights every afternoon, didn't you?"

"You can't play in the dark," he answered gruffly.

"And you swept away the puddles on rainy days."

This time he only nodded.

"I know who you are," River said. "I know exactly who you are."

Rochelle was very quiet, watching.

Kammie said, "Who?! Who is he?"

"He's the Basketball Court Goddess!"

River gave Coach Glover a big hug. She could tell he wasn't very used to hugs. He just stood there, stiffly, with his arms at his side.

"You're a good coach," River told him. "But my brother's a better one."

Coach Glover actually smiled then.

"Tomorrow," River said to Rochelle. "Right after school, in your new haunted house. Hoops. Okay?"

Rochelle smiled, too.

River and Kammie decided to walk home, and they started down the road in the early dusk. The sky had deepened to lavender. River's body felt good with that looseness that comes only after playing a great game of basketball.

When they reached the timber baron's house, now the Glovers' house, Kammie stopped. She asked, "What secret door did you go through?"

River shrugged.

"You said that when you drove through the key those times and made those great shots, that you weren't mad. You said you went through a secret door."

"Yeah. I guess so."

"What secret door?"

"You wouldn't understand."

"You want to keep it secret so that no one else can go through the door?"

"No, that's not it."

"Then tell me."

"It's the opposite of getting mad. Everything becomes a flow. The basketball and hoop are all I can see. It's like one minute I'm in this world, and then I step through a door and I'm in the magical kingdom of basketball."

"How do you find the secret door?"

"I don't know. It just . . . is suddenly there."

Kammie looked thoughtful for a second, and then said, "I'd rather get mad. But with your secret door and my killer instinct, we'll definitely win next time."

"You and me?" River said quietly but fiercely. "When we hit the WNBA, we're gonna kick butt."

LUCY JANE BLEDSOE has written three previous books for children: *The Big Bike Race, Cougar Canyon,* and *Tracks in the Snow*, which appeared on six state award lists and received a Parent's Choice Gold Award. An avid athlete, she bikes, hikes, skis, and mountain climbs. Her next novel takes place in Antarctica, where she traveled for three months as a recipient of a National Science Foundation Artists & Writers Grant.